"Will you marry me, Sophie?"

Her smile melted into a look of utter surprise. "Marry you? Why? Whatever for?"

Rijk smiled at that. "We are good friends. Have we not just agreed about that? We enjoy doing the same things, we laugh at the same things.... I want someone to share my life, Sophie, a companion, someone to make my house a home."

She met his intent look honestly, although her cheeks were pink. "But we don't—that is, shouldn't there be love, as well?"

Betty Neels is well-known for her romances set in the Netherlands, which is hardly surprising. She married a Dutchman and spent the first twelve years of their marriage living in Holland and working as a nurse. Today, she and her husband make their home in an ancient stone cottage in England's West Country, but they return to Holland often. She loves to explore tiny villages and tour privately owned homes there in order to lend an air of authenticity to the background of her books.

Books by Betty Neels

Don't miss any of our special offers. Write to us at the following address for information on our newest releases.

Harlequin Reader Service
U.S.: 3010 Walden Ave., P.O. Box 1325, Buffalo, NY 14269
Canadian: P.O. Box 609, Fort Erie, Ont. L2A 5X3

THE AWAKENED HEART
Betty Neels

Harlequin Books

TORONTO • NEW YORK • LONDON
AMSTERDAM • PARIS • SYDNEY • HAMBURG
STOCKHOLM • ATHENS • TOKYO • MILAN
MADRID • WARSAW • BUDAPEST • AUCKLAND

ISBN 0-373-03339-7

THE AWAKENED HEART

This edition published by arrangement with Harlequin Enterprises B.V.

® and TM are trademarks of the publisher. Trademarks indicated with ® are registered in the United States Patent and Trademark Office, the Canadian Trade Marks Office and in other countries.

Printed in U.S.A.

CHAPTER ONE

THE dull October afternoon was fast becoming a damp evening, its drizzling rain soaking those hurrying home from work. The pavements were crowded; the wholesale dress shops, the shabby second-hand-furniture emporiums, the small businesses carried on behind dirty shop windows were all closing for the day. There were still one or two street barrows doing a desultory trade, but the street, overshadowed by the great bulk of St Agnes's hospital, in an hour or so's time would be almost empty. Just at the moment it was alive with those intent on getting home, with the exception of one person: a tall girl, standing still, a look of deep concentration on her face, oblivious of the impatient jostling her splendid person was receiving from passers-by.

Unnoticed by those jostling her, she was none the less attracting the attention of a man standing at the window of the committee-room of the hospital overlooking the street. He watched her for several minutes, at first idly and then with a faint frown, and presently, since he had nothing better to do for the moment, he made his way out of the hospital across the forecourt and into the street.

The girl was on the opposite pavement and he crossed the road without haste, a giant of a man with wide shoulders, making light of the crowds around him. His

'Can I be of help?' was asked in a quiet, deep voice, and the girl looked at him with relief.

'So silly,' she said in a matter-of-fact voice. 'The heel of my shoe is wedged in a gutter and my hands are full. If you would be so kind as to hold these...'

She handed him two plastic shopping-bags. 'They're lace-ups,' she explained. 'I can't get my foot out.'

The size of him had caused passers-by to make a little detour around them. He handed back the bags. 'Allow me?' he begged her and crouched down, unlaced her shoe, and when she had got her foot out of it carefully worked the heel free, held it while she put her foot back in, and tied the laces tidily.

She thanked him then, smiling up into his handsome face, to be taken aback by the frosty blue of his eyes and his air of cool detachment, rather as though he had been called upon to do something which he had found tiresome. Well, perhaps it had been tiresome, but surely he didn't have to look at her like that? He was smiling now too, a small smile which just touched his firm mouth and gave her the nasty feeling that he knew just what she was thinking. She removed the smile, flashed him a look from beautiful dark eyes, wished him goodbye, and joined the hurrying crowd around her. He had ruffled her feelings, although she wasn't sure why. She dismissed him from her mind and turned into a side-street lined with old-fashioned houses with basements guarded by iron railings badly in need of paint; the houses were slightly down at heel too and the variety of curtains at their windows bore testimony to the fact that subletting was the norm.

Halfway down the street she mounted the steps of a house rather better kept than its neighbours and unlocked the door. The hall was narrow and rather dark and redolent of several kinds of cooking. The girl wrinkled her beautiful nose and started up the stairs, to be stopped by a voice from a nearby room.

'Is that you, Sister Blount? There was a phone call for you...'

A middle-aged face, crowned by a youthful blonde wig, appeared round the door. 'Your dear mother, wishing to speak to you. I was so bold as to tell her that you would be home at six o'clock.'

The girl paused on the stairs. 'Thank you, Miss Phipps. I'll phone as soon as I've been to my room.'

Miss Phipps frowned and then decided to be playfully rebuking. 'Your flatlet, Sister, dear. I flatter myself that my tenants are worthy of something better than bed-sitting-rooms.'

The girl murmured and smiled and went up two flights of stairs to the top floor and unlocked the only door on the small landing. It was an attic room with the advantage of a window overlooking the street as well as a smaller one which gave a depressing view of back yards and strings of washing, but there was a tree by it where sparrows sat, waiting for the crumbs on the window sill. It had a wash-basin in one corner and a small gas stove in an alcove by the blocked-up fireplace. There was a small gas fire too, and these, according to Miss Phipps, added up to mod cons and a flatlet. The bathroom was shared too by the two flatlets on the floor below, but since she was on night duty and everyone else worked during the day that was no problem. She dumped her shopping on the small table under the window, took off her coat, kicked off her shoes, stuck her feet into slippers and bent to pick up the small tabby cat which had uncurled itself from the end of the divan bed against one wall.

'Mabel, hello. I'll be back in a moment to get your supper...'

The phone was in the hall and to hold a private conversation on it was impossible, for Miss Phipps rarely shut her door. She fed the machine some ten-pence pieces and dialled her home.

'Sophie?' her `mother's voice answered at once. 'Darling, it isn't anything important; I just wanted to know how you were and when you're coming home for a day or two.'

'I was coming at the end of the week, but Sister Symonds is ill again. She should be back by the end of next week, though, and I'll take two lots of nights off at once—almost a week...'

'Oh, good. Let us know which train and someone will pick you up at the station. You're busy?'

'Yes, off and on—not too bad.' Sophie always said that. She was always busy; Casualty and the accident room took no account of time of day or night. She knew that her mother thought of her as sitting for a great part of the night at the tidy desk, giving advice and from time to time checking on a more serious case, and Sophie hadn't enlightened her. On really busy nights she hardly saw her desk at all, but, sleeves rolled up and plastic apron tied around her slim waist, she worked wherever she was most needed.

'Is that Miss Phipps listening?'

'Of course...'

'What would happen if you brought a man back for supper?' Her mother chuckled.

'When do I ever get the time?' asked Sophie and allowed her thoughts to dwell just for a moment on the man with the cold blue eyes. The sight of her flatlet would trigger off the little smile; she had no doubt of that. Probably he had never seen anything like it in his life.

They didn't talk for long; conversation wasn't easy with Miss Phipps's wig just visible in the crack of her door. Sophie hung up and went upstairs, fed Mabel and opened the window which gave on to a railed-off ledge so that the little beast could air herself, and put away her shopping. What with one thing and another, there was barely time for her to get a meal before she went on duty. She made a pot of tea, opened a tin of beans, poached an egg, and did her face and hair again. Her face, she reflected, staring at it in the old-fashioned looking-glass on the wall above the basin, looked tired. 'I shall have wrinkles and lines before I know where I am,' said Sophie to Mabel, watching her from the bed.

Nonsense, of course; she was blessed with a lovely face: wide dark eyes, a delightful nose above a gentle, generous mouth, and long, curling lashes as dark as her hair, long and thick and worn in a complicated arrangement which took quite a time to do but which stayed tidy however busy she was.

She stooped to drop a kiss on the cat's head, picked up her roomy shoulder-bag, and let herself out of the room, a tall girl with a splendid figure and beautiful legs.

Her flatlet might lack the refinements of home, but it was only five minutes' walk from the hospital. She crossed the courtyard with five minutes to spare, watched, if she did but know, by the man who had retrieved her shoe for her—in the committee-room again, exchanging a desultory conversation with those of his colleagues who were lingering after their meeting. Tomorrow would be a busy day, for he had come over to England especially to operate on a cerebral tumour; brain surgery was something on which he was an acknowledged expert, so that a good deal of his work was international. Already famous in his own country, he was fast attaining the highest rung of the ladder.

He stood now, looking from the window, studying Sophie's splendid person as she crossed the forecourt.

'Who is that?' he asked Dr Wells, the anaesthetist who would be working with him in the morning and an old friend.

'That's our Sophie, Night Sister in Casualty and the accident room, worth her not inconsiderable weight in gold too. Pretty girl...'

They parted company presently and Professor Rijk van Taak ter Wijsma made his way without haste down to the entrance. He was stopped before he reached it by the surgical registrar who was to assist him in the morning, so that they were both deep in talk when the first of the ambulances flashed past on its way to the accident room entrance.

They were still discussing the morning's work when the registrar's bleep interrupted them.

He listened for a minute and said, 'There's a head injury in, Professor—contusion and laceration with evidence of coning. Mr Bellamy had planned a weekend off...'

His companion took his phone from him and dialled a number. 'Hello, John? Rijk here. Peter Small is here with me; they want him in the accident room—there's a head injury just in. As I'm here, shall I take a look? I know you're not on call...' He listened for a moment. 'Good, we'll go along and have a look.'

He gave the phone back. 'You wouldn't mind if I took a look? There might be something I could suggest...'

'That's very good of you, sir; you don't mind?'

'Not in the least.'

The accident room was busy, but then it almost always was. Sophie, with a practised glance at the patient, sent the junior sister to deal with the less urgent cases with the aid of two student nurses, taking the third nurse with her as the paramedics wheeled the patient into an empty cubicle. The casualty officer was already there; while he phoned the registrar they began connecting up the various monitoring tubes and checked the oxygen flow, working methodically and with the sure speed of long practice. All the same, she could see that the man on the stretcher was in a bad way.

She was trying to count an almost imperceptible pulse when she became conscious of someone standing just behind her and then edging her gently to one side while a large, well kept hand gently lifted the dressing on the battered head.

'Tut, tut,' said the professor. 'What do we know, Sister?'

'A fall from a sixth-floor window on to a concrete pavement. Thready pulse, irregular and slow, cerebrospinal fluid from left ear, epistaxis...'

Her taxing training was standing her in good stead; she answered him promptly and with few words, while a small part of her mind registered the fact that the man beside her had tied her shoelaces for her not two hours since.

What a small world, she reflected, and allowed herself a second's pleasure at seeing him again. But only a second; she was already busy adjusting tubes and knobs at the registrar's low-voiced instructions.

The two men bent over the unconscious patient while she took a frighteningly high blood-pressure and the casualty officer looked for other injuries and broken bones.

Presently the professor straightened up. 'Anterior fossa—depressed fracture. Let's have an X-ray and get him up to Theatre.' He took a look at Peter Small. 'You agree? There's a good chance...' He glanced at Sophie. 'If you would warn Theatre, Sister? Thank you.'

He gave her a brief look; he didn't recognise her, thought Sophie, but then why should he? She was in uniform now, the old-fashioned dark blue dress and frilly cap which St Agnes's management committee refused to exchange for nylon and paper.

The men went away, leaving her to organise the patient's removal to the theatre block, warn Night Theatre Sister, Intensive Care and the men's surgical ward, and, that done, there was the business of his identity, his address, his family... It was going to be a busy night, Sophie decided, writing and telephoning, dealing with everything and the police, and at the same time keeping an eye on the incoming patients. Nothing too serious from a medical point of view, although bad enough for the owners of sprained ankles, cut heads, fractured arms and legs, but they all needed attention— X-rays, cleaning and stitching and bandaging, and sometimes admitting to a ward.

It was two o'clock in the morning, and she had just wolfed down a sandwich and drunk a reviving mug of tea since there had been no chance of getting down to the canteen, when a girl was brought in, a small toddler screaming her head off in her mother's arms, who thrust her at Sophie. ''Ere, take a look at 'er, will yer? Fell down the stairs, been bawling 'er 'ead off ever since.'

Sophie laid the grubby scrap gently on to one of the couches. 'How long ago was this?'

The woman shrugged. 'Dunno. Me neighbour told me when I got 'ome—nine o'clock, I suppose.'

Sophie was examining the little girl gently. 'She had got out of her bed?'

'Bed? She don't go ter bed till I'm 'ome.'

Sophie sent a nurse to see if she could fetch the casualty officer and, when she found him and he arrived, left the nurse with him and ushered the mother into her office.

'I shall want your name and address and the little girl's name. How was she able to get to the stairs? Is it a high-rise block of flats?' She glanced at the address again. 'At the end of Montrose Street, isn't it?'

'S'right, fifth floor. I leave the door, see, so's me neighbour can take a look at Tracey...'

'She is left alone during the day?'

'Well, off and on, you might say, and sometimes of an evening—just when I go to the pub evenings.'

'Well, shall we see what the doctor says? Perhaps it may be necessary to keep Tracey in the hospital for a day or two.'

'Suits me—driving me mad with that howling, she is.'

Tracey had stopped crying; only an occasional snivel betrayed her misery. Sophie said briskly, 'You'd like her admitted for observation, Dr Wright?' and at the same time bestowed a warning frown on him; Jeff Wright and she had been friends for ages, and he understood the frown.

'Oh, definitely, Sister, if you would arrange it. This is the mother?' He bent an earnest gaze upon the woman, who said at once,

'It ain't my fault. I've got ter 'ave a bit of fun, 'aven't I? Me 'usband left me, see?'

Sophie thought that he might have good reason. The woman was dirty, and although she was wearing make-up and cheap fashionable clothes the child was in a smelly dress and vest and no nappy. 'You may visit when you like,' she told her. 'Would you like to stay until she is settled in?'

'No, thanks. I gotta get some sleep, haven't I?'

She nodded to the child. 'Bye for now, night all.'

'Be an angel and right away get the children's ward,' said Sophie. 'I'll wrap this scrap up in a blanket and take her up—a pity we can't clean her up first, but I can't spare the nurses.'

All the same, she wiped the small grubby face and peeled off the outer layer of garments before cuddling Tracey into a blanket and picking her up carefully. There were no bones broken, luckily, but a great deal of bruising, and in the morning the paediatrician would go over the small body and make sure that no great harm had been done.

She took the lift and got out at the third floor and walked straight into the professor's vast person. He was alone and still in his theatre gear.

'Having a busy night, Sister?' he asked, in a far too cheerful voice for the small hours.

Her 'Yes, sir' was terse, and he smiled.

'Hardly the best of times in which to renew an acquaintance, is it?' He stood on one side so that she might pass. 'We must hope for a more fortunate meeting.'

Sophie hoisted the sleeping toddler a little higher against her shoulder. She was tired and wanted a cup of tea and a chance to sit down for ten minutes; she was certainly not in a mood for polite conversation.

'Unlikely,' she observed crossly. She had gone several steps when she paused and turned to look at him.

'That man—you've operated?'

'Yes; given a modicum of luck and some good nursing, he should recover.'

'Oh, I'm so glad.' She nodded and went on her way, her busy night somehow worth while at the news.

The senior sister, when she came on duty in the morning, was full of complaints. She was on the wrong side of forty and an habitual grumbler; Sophie, listening with inward impatience to peevish criticisms about the weather, breakfast, the rudeness of student nurses and the impossibility of finding the shoes she wanted, choked back a yawn and presently took herself thankfully off duty.

Breakfast was always a cheerful meal, despite the fact that they were all tired; Sophie poured herself a cup of tea, collected a substantial plateful of food, and sat down with the other night sisters. There was quite a tableful, and despite the fact that they were all weary the conversation was lively.

Theatre Sister held the attention of the whole table almost at once. 'We scrubbed at nine o'clock and didn't finish until after two in the morning. There was this super man operating—Professor something or other. He's from Holland—a pal of Mr Bellamy's—and over here to demonstrate some new technique. He made a marvellous job of this poor chap too.'

She beamed round the table, a small waif of a girl with big blue eyes and fair hair. 'He's a smasher—my dears, you should just see him. Enormous and very tall, blue eyes and very fair hair, nicely grey at the sides. He's operating again at ten o'clock and when Sister Tucker heard about him she said she'd scrub...'

There was a ripple of laughter; Sister Tucker was getting on a bit and as theatre superintendent very seldom took a case. 'Bet you wish you were on duty, Gill,' said someone and then, 'What about you, Sophie? Did you see this marvellous man?'

Sophie bit into her toast. 'Yes, he came into the accident room with Peter Small—I believe he's just arrived here.' She took another bite and her companions asked impatiently,

'Well, what's he like? Did you take a good look...?'

'Not really; he's tall and large...' She glanced round her. 'There wasn't much chance...'

'Oh, hard luck, and you're not likely to see him again—Gill's the lucky one.'

'Who's got nights off?' someone asked.

The lucky ones were quick to say, and someone said, 'And you, Sophie? Aren't you due this weekend?'

'Yes, but Ida Symonds is ill again, so I'll have to do her weekend. Never mind, I shall take a whole week when she comes back.' She put up a shapely hand to cover a yawn. 'I'm for bed.'

They left the table in twos and threes and went along to the changing-room and presently went their various ways. The professor, on the point of getting out of the silver-grey Bentley he had parked in the forecourt, watched Sophie come out of the entrance, reach the street and cross over before he got out of the car and made his unhurried way to the theatre, where Sister Tucker awaited him.

Sophie, in her flatlet, making a cup of tea and seeing to Mabel's breakfast, found herself thinking about the professor; she was unwilling to admit it, but she would like to meet him again. Perhaps, she thought guiltily, she had been a bit rude when they had met on her way to the children's ward. And why had he said that he hoped for a more fortunate meeting?

She wasn't a conceited girl, but she knew that she was nice-looking—she was too big to be called pretty and, though she was, she had never thought of herself as beautiful. She never lacked invitations to go out with the house doctors, something she occasionally did, but she was heart-whole and content to stay as she was until the right man came along. Only just lately she had had one or two uneasy twinges about that; she had had several proposals and refused them in the nicest possible way, waiting for the vague and unknown dream man who would sweep her off her feet and leave no room for doubts...

Presently she went to bed with Mabel for company and slept at once, ignoring the good advice offered by her landlady, who considered that a brisk walk before bed was the correct thing to do for those who were on night duty. That she had never been on night duty in her life and had no idea what that entailed was beside the point. Besides, the East End of London was hardly conducive to a walk, especially when there was still a faint drizzle left over from the day before.

Sophie wakened refreshed, took a bath, attended to Mabel, and, still in her dressing-gown, made a pot of tea and sat down by the gas fire to enjoy it. She had taken the first delicious sip when someone knocked at the door.

Sophie put down her cup and muttered crossly at Mabel, who muttered back. Miss Phipps, a deeply suspicious person, collected her rent weekly, and it was Friday. Sophie picked up her purse and opened the door.

Only it wasn't Miss Phipps; it was Professor van Taak ter Wijsma.

She opened her mouth, but before she could utter a squeak he laid a finger upon it.

'Your good landlady,' said the professor in a voice strong enough to be heard by that lady lurking at the bottom of the stairs, 'has kindly allowed me to visit you on a matter of some importance.' As he spoke he pushed her gently back into the room and closed the door behind them both...

'Well,' said Sophie with a good deal of heat, 'what in heaven's name are you doing here? Go away at once.' She remembered that she was still in her dressing-gown, a rather fetching affair in quilted rose-pink satin. 'I'm not dressed ...'

'I had noticed, but let me assure you that since I have five sisters girls in dressing-gowns hold no surprises for me.' He added thoughtfully, 'Although I must admit that this one becomes you very well.'

'What's so important?' snapped Sophie. 'I can't imagine what it can be.'

'No, no, how could you?' He spoke soothingly. 'I am going to Liverpool tomorrow and I shall be back on Wednesday. I thought that a drive into the country when you come off duty might do you good—fresh air, you know... I'll have to have you back here by one o'clock and you can go straight to bed.'

He was strolling around the room, looking at everything. 'Why do you live in this terrible room with that even more terrible woman who is your landlady?'

'Because it's close to the hospital and I can't afford anything better.' She added, 'Oh, do go away. I can't think why you came.'

'Why, to tell you that I will pick you up on Wednesday morning—from here?—and take you for an airing. Your temper will be improved by a peaceful drive.'

She stood in front of him, trying to find the right words, so that she could tell him just what she thought of him, but she couldn't think of them. He said gently, 'I'll be here at half-past nine.' He had picked up Mabel, who had settled her small furry head against his shoulder, purring with pleasure.

Sophie had the outrageous thought that the shoulder would be very nice to lean against; she had the feeling that she was standing in a strong wind and being blown somewhere. She heard herself saying, 'Oh, all right, but I can't think why. And do go; I'm on duty in half an hour...'

'I'll be downstairs waiting for you; we can walk back together. Don't be long, for I think that I shall find Miss Phipps a trying conversationalist.'

He let himself out, leaving her to dress rapidly, do her hair and face, and make suitable arrangements for Mabel's comfort during the night, and while she did that she thought about the professor. An arrogant type, she told herself, used to having influence and his own way and doubtless having his every whim pandered to. Just because he had happened to be there when she'd needed help with that wretched shoe didn't mean that he could scrape acquaintance with her. 'I shall tell him that I have changed my mind,' she told Mabel. 'There is absolutely no reason why I should go out with him.'

She put the little cat in her basket, picked up her shoulder-bag, and went downstairs.

Miss Phipps, pink-cheeked and wig slightly askew, was talking animatedly to the professor, describing with a wealth of detail just how painful were her bunions. The professor, who had had nothing to do with bunions for years, listened courteously, and gravely advised a visit to her own doctor. Then he bade her an equally courteous goodnight and swept Sophie out into the damp darkness.

'I dislike this road,' he observed, taking her arm.

For some reason his arm worried her. She said, knowing that she was being rude, 'Well, you don't have to live in it, do you?'

His answer brought her up short. 'My poor girl, you should be living in the country—open fields and hedgerows...'

'Well, I do,' she said waspishly. 'My home is in the country.'

'You do not wish to work near your home?' The question was put so casually that she answered without thinking.

'Well, that would be splendid, but it's miles from anywhere. Besides, I can get there easily enough from here.'

He didn't comment on her unconscious contradiction, and since they were already in the forecourt of St Agnes's he made some remark about the hospital and, once inside its doors, bade her a civil goodnight and went away in the direction of the consultant's room.

In the changing-room, full of night sisters getting into their uniforms, she heard Gill's voice from the further end. 'He's been operating for most of the day,' she was saying. 'I dare say he'll have a look at his patients this evening—men's surgical. I shall make an excuse to go down there to borrow something. Kitty——' Kitty was the night sister there '—give me a ring when he does. He's going away tomorrow, did you know?' She addressed her companions at large. 'But he'll be back.'

'How do you know?' someone asked.

'Oh, I phoned Theatre Sister earlier this evening—had a little gossip...'

They all laughed, and although Sophie laughed too she felt a bit guilty, but somehow she couldn't bring

herself to tell them about her unexpected visitor tha
evening, nor the conversation she had had with him. She
didn't think anyone would believe her anyway. She wasn'
sure if she believed it herself.

Several busy nights brought her to Wednesday mornin₽
and the realisation that since she hadn't seen the pro
fessor she hadn't been able to refuse to go out with him
'I shall do so if and when he comes,' she told Mabel
who went on cleaning her whiskers, quite unconcerned

Sophie had had far too busy a night and she potterec
rather grumpily around her room, not sure whether t
have her bath first or a soothing cup of tea. She hac
neither. Miss Phipps, possibly scenting romance, climbec
the stairs to tell her that she was wanted on the phone
'That nice gentleman,' she giggled, 'said I was to get you
out of the bath if necessary.' She caught Sophie's fulmi
nating eye and added hastily, 'Just his little joke; gentle
men do like their little jokes...'

Sophie choked back a rude answer and went down
stairs, closely followed by her landlady, who, althougl
she went into her room, took care to leave the door
slightly open.

'Hello,' said Sophie in her haughtiest voice.

'As cross as two sticks,' answered the professor':
placid voice. 'I shall be with you in exactly ten minutes.

He hung up before she could utter a word. She pu
the receiver back and the phone rang again and wher
she picked it up he said, 'If you aren't at the door I shal
come up for you. Don't worry, I'll bring Miss Phipp₅
with me as a chaperon.'

Sophie thumped down the receiver once more, ig
nored Miss Phipps's inquisitive face peering round her

door, and took herself back to her room. 'I don't want to go out,' she told Mabel. 'It's the very last thing I want to do.'

All the same, she did things to her face and hair and put on her coat, assured Mabel that she wouldn't be away for long, and went downstairs again with a minute to spare.

The professor was already there, exchanging small talk with Miss Phipps, who gave Sophie an awfully sickening roguish look and said something rather muddled about pretty girls not needing beauty sleep if there was something better to do. Sophie cast her a look of outrage and bade the professor a frosty good morning, leaving him to make his polite goodbyes to her landlady, before she was swept out into the chilly morning and into the Bentley's welcoming warmth.

It was disconcerting when he remained silent, driving the car out of London on the A12 and, once clear of the straggling suburbs, turning off on to a side-road into the Essex countryside, presently turning off again on to an even smaller road, apparently leading to nowhere.

'Feeling better?' he asked her.

'Yes,' said Sophie, and added, 'Thank you.'

'Do you know this part of the world?' His voice was quiet.

'No, at least not the side-roads; it's not as quick...' She stopped just in time.

'I suppose it's quicker for you to turn off at Romford and go through Chipping Ongar?'

She turned to look at him, but he was gazing ahead, his profile calm.

'How did you know where I live?' She had been comfortably somnolent, but now she was wide awake.

'I asked Peter Small; do you mind?'

'Mind? I don't know; I can't think why you should want to know. Were you just being curious?'

'No, no, I never give way to idle curiosity. Now if I'm right there's a nice little pub in the next village—we might get coffee there.'

The pub was charming, clean and rather bare, with not a fruit machine in sight. There was a log fire smouldering in the vast stone fireplace, with an elderly dog stretched out before it, and the landlord, pleased to have custom before the noonday locals arrived, offered a plate of hot buttered toast to devour with the coffee.

Biting into her third slice, Sophie asked, 'Why did you want to know?' Mellowed by the toast and the coffee, she felt strangely friendly towards her companion.

'I'm not sure if you would believe me if I told you. Shall I say that, despite a rather unsettled start, I feel that we might become friends?'

'What would be the point? I mean, we don't move in the same circles, do we? You live in Holland—don't you?—and I live here. Besides, we don't know anything about each other.'

'Exactly. It behoves us to remedy that, does it not? You have nights off at the weekend? I'll drive you home.'

'Drive me home,' repeated Sophie, parrot-fashion. 'But what am I to say to Mother...?'

'My dear girl, don't tell me that you haven't been taken home by any number of young men...'

'Well, yes, but you're different.'

'Older?' He smiled suddenly and she discovered that she liked him more than she had thought. 'Confess that you feel better, Sophie; you need some male companionship—nothing serious, just a few pleasant hours from time to time. After all, as you said, I live in Holland.'

'Are you married?'

He laughed gently. 'No, Sophie—and you?'

She shook her head and smiled dazzlingly. 'It would be nice to have a casual friend... I'm not sure how I feel. Do we know each other well enough for me to go to sleep on the way back?'

CHAPTER TWO

So SOPHIE slept, her mouth slightly open, her head lolling on the professor's shoulder, to be gently roused at Miss Phipps's door, eased out of the car, still not wholly awake, and ushered into the house.

'Thank you very much,' said Sophie. 'That was a very nice ride.' She stared up at him, her eyes huge in her tired face.

'Is ten o'clock too early for you on Saturday?'

'No. Mabel has to come too...'

'Of course. Sleep well, Sophie.'

He propelled her gently to the stairs and watched her climb them and was in turn watched by Miss Phipps through her half-open door. When he heard Sophie's door shut he wished a slightly flustered Miss Phipps good morning and took himself off.

Sophie told herself that it was a change of scene which had made her feel so pleased with life. She woke up with the pleasant feeling that something nice had happened. True, the professor had made some rather strange remarks, and perhaps she had said rather more than she had intended, but her memory was a little hazy, for she had been very tired, and there was no use worrying about that now. It would be delightful to be driven home on Saturday...

Casualty was busy when she went on duty that evening, but there was nothing very serious and nothing at all in the accident room; she went to her midnight meal so punctually that various of her friends commented upon it.

'What's happened to you, Sophie?' asked Gill. 'You look as though you've won the pools.'

'Or fallen in love,' said someone from the other side of the table. 'Who is it, Sophie?'

'Neither—I had a good sleep, and it's a quiet night, thank heaven.'

'If you say so,' said Gill. 'I haven't won the pools—something much more exciting. That lovely man is operating at eight o'clock tomorrow morning. I have offered to lay up for Sister Tucker——' there was a burst of laughter '—just so that everything would be ready for him, and I shan't mind if I'm a few minutes late off duty.' She smiled widely. 'Especially if I should happen to bump into him.'

Joan Middleton, in charge of men's medical, the only one of them who was married and therefore not particularly interested, observed in her matter-of-fact way, 'Probably he's married with half a dozen children—he's not all that young, is he?'

'He's not even middle-aged,' said Gill sharply. 'Sophie, you've seen him. He's still quite young—in his thirties, wouldn't you think?'

Sophie looked vague. 'Probably.' She took another piece of toast and reached for the marmalade.

Gill said happily, 'Well, I dare say he falls for little wistful women, like me...' And although Sophie laughed with the rest of them, she didn't feel too sure about that. No, that wouldn't do at all, she reflected. Just because he had taken her for a drive didn't mean that he had any interest in her; indeed, it might be a cunning way of covering his real interest in Gill, who, after all, was exactly the type of girl a man would fall for. Never mind that she was the soul of efficiency in Theatre; once out of uniform, she became helpless, wistful and someone to be cherished. Helplessness and wistfulness didn't sit happily on Sophie.

Sophie saw nothing of the professor for the few nights left before she was due for nights off. She heard a good deal about him, though, for Gill had contrived to waylay him in Theatre before she went off duty and was full of his good looks and charm; moreover, when she went on duty the following night there had been an emergency operation and he was still in Theatre, giving her yet another chance to exchange a few words with him.

'I wonder where he goes for his weekends?' said Gill, looking round the breakfast-table.

Sophie, who could have told her, remained silent; instead she observed that she was off home just as soon as she could get changed, bade everyone goodbye, and took herself off.

She showered and changed into a rather nice multi-check jacket in a dark red with its matching skirt, tucked a cream silk scarf in the neck, stuck her feet into low-heeled black shoes, and, with her face carefully made-up and her hair in its complicated coil, took herself to the long mirror inside the old-fashioned wardrobe and had an appraising look.

'Not too bad,' she remarked to Mabel as she popped her into her travel basket, slung her simple weekend bag over her shoulder, and went down to the front door. It was ten o'clock, and she didn't allow herself to think what she would do if he wasn't there...

He was, sitting in his magnificent car, reading a news-paper. He got out as she opened the door, rather ham-pered by Miss Phipps, who was quite unnecessarily holding it open for her, bade her good morning, took Mabel, who was grumbling to herself in her basket, wished Miss Phipps good day, and stowed both Sophie and Mabel into his car without further ado. He achieved this with a courteous speed which rather took Sophie's breath, but as he drove away she said severely, 'Good morning, Professor.'

'I suspect that you are put out at my businesslike greeting. That can be improved upon later. I felt it necessary to get away quickly before that tiresome woman began a conversation; I find her exhausting.'

An honest girl, Sophie said at once, 'I'm not put out; at least, I wasn't quite sure that you would be here. As for Miss Phipps, I expect she's lonely.'

'That I find hard to believe; what I find even harder to believe is that you doubted my word.' He glanced sideways at her. 'I told you that I would be outside your lodgings at ten o'clock.'

'I don't think I doubted you,' she said slowly. 'I think I wasn't quite sure why you were giving me a lift—I mean it's out of your way, isn't it?'

'I make a point of seeing as much of the English countryside as possible when I am over here.'

She wasn't sure whether that was a gentle snub or not; in any case she wasn't sure how to answer it, so she made a remark about the weather and he replied suitably and they lapsed into a silence broken only by Mabel's gentle grumbling from the back seat.

Sophie, left to her thoughts, wondered what would be the best thing to do when they arrived at her home. Should she ask him in for coffee or merely thank him for the lift and allow him to go to wherever he was going? She had phoned her mother on the previous evening and told her that she was getting a lift home, but she hadn't said much else...

'Would you like to stop for coffee or do you suppose your mother would be kind enough to have it ready for us?'

It was as though he had known just what she had been thinking. 'I'm sure she will expect us in time for coffee—that is, if you would like to stop...'

'I should like to meet your parents.' He sounded friendly, and she was emboldened to ask, 'How long will you be in England?'

'I shall go back to Holland in a couple of weeks.'

A remark which left her feeling strangely forlorn.

They were clear of the eastern suburbs by now and he turned off on to the road to Chipping Ongar. The countryside was surprisingly rural once they left the main road and when he took a small side-road before they reached that town she said in surprise, 'Oh, you know this part of the country?'

'Only from my map. I find it delightful that one can leave the main roads so easily and get comfortably lost in country lanes.'

'Can't you do that in Holland?'

'Not easily. The country is flat, so that there is always a town or a village on the horizon.' He added to surprise her, 'What do you intend to do with your life, Sophie?'

'Me?' The question was so unexpected that she hadn't a ready answer. 'Well, I've a good job at St Agnes's ...'

'No boyfriend, no thought of marriage?'

'No.'

'And it's none of my business ...' he laughed. 'Tell me, is it quicker to go through Cooksmill Green or take the road on the left at the next crossroads?'

'If you were on your own it would be best to go through Cooksmill Green, but since I'm here to show you the way go left; there aren't any villages until we get to Shellow Roding.'

It really was rural now, with wide fields on either side of the road bordered by trees and thick hedges, and presently the spire of the village church came into view and the first of the cottages, their ochre or white walls crowned by thatch, thickening into clusters on either side of the green with the church at one side of it, the village pub opposite and a row of small neat shops.

'Charming,' observed the professor and, obedient to Sophie's instruction, turned the car down a narrow lane beside the church.

Her home was a few hundred yards beyond. The house was old and bore the mark of several periods, its colour-washed walls pierced by a variety of windows. A stone wall, crumbling in places, surrounded the garden, and an open gate to the short drive led them to the front door.

The professor brought the car to a silent halt, and got out to open Sophie's door and reach on to the back seat

for Mabel's basket, and at the same time the door opened
and Sophie's mother came out to meet them. She was a
tall woman, as splendidly built as her daughter, her dark
hair streaked with grey, her face still beautiful. Two dogs
followed her, a Jack Russell and a whippet, both barking
and cruising round Sophie.

'Darling,' said Mrs Blount, 'how lovely to see you.'
She gave Sophie a kiss and turned to the professor,
smiling.

'Mother, this is Professor van Taak ter Wijsma, who
has kindly given me a lift. My mother, Professor.'

'A professor,' observed Mrs Blount. 'I dare say you're
frightfully clever?' She smiled at him, liking what she
saw. Really, thought Sophie, he had only to smile like
that and everyone fell for him. But not me, she added,
silently careless of grammar; we're just friends...

Mrs Blount led the way indoors. 'A pity the boys aren't
at home; they'd have loved your big motor car.'

'Perhaps another time,' murmured the professor. He
somehow conveyed the impression that he knew the
entire family well—was an old friend, in fact. Sophie let
Mabel out of her basket, feeling put out, although she
had no idea why. There was no time to dwell on that,
however. The dogs, Montgomery and Mercury, recog-
nising Mabel as a well established visitor, were intent on
a game, and by the time Sophie had quietened them down
everyone had settled down in the kitchen, a large, cosy
room, warm from the Aga, the vast dresser loaded with
a variety of dishes and plates, the large table in its centre
ringed by old-fashioned wooden chairs. There was a bowl
of apples on it and a plate of scones, and a coffee-pot,
equally old-fashioned, sat on the Aga.

'So much warmer in the kitchen,' observed Mrs Blount breezily, 'though if I had known who you were I would have had the best china out in the drawing-room.'

'Professors are ten a penny,' he assured her, 'and this is a delightful room.'

Sophie had taken off her coat and come to sit at the table. 'Do you work together at St Agnes's?' asked her mother.

'Our paths cross from time to time, do they not, Sophie?'

'I'm on night duty,' said Sophie quite unnecessarily. She passed him the scones, and since they were both looking at her she added, 'If there's a case—Professor van Taak ter Wijsma is a brain surgeon.'

'You don't live here, do you?' asked Mrs Blount as she refilled his coffee-mug.

'No, no, my home is normally in Holland, but I travel around a good deal.'

'A pity your father isn't at home, Sophie; he would have enjoyed meeting Professor van Taak...' She paused. 'I've forgotten the rest of it; I am sorry.'

'Please call me Rijk; it is so much easier. Perhaps I shall have the pleasure of meeting your husband at some time, Mrs Blount.'

'Oh, I do hope so. He's a vet, you know; he has a surgery here in the village and is senior partner at the veterinary centre in Chipping Ongar. He's always busy...'

Sophie drank her coffee, not saying much. The professor had wormed his way into her family with ease, she reflected crossly. It was all very well, all his talk about being friends, but she wasn't going to be rushed into anything, not even the casual friendship he had spoken of.

He got up to go presently, shook Mrs Blount's hand, dropped a casual kiss on Sophie's cheek with the remark that he would call for her on Sunday next week about eight o'clock, and got into his car and drove away. He left Sophie red in the face and speechless and her mother thoughtful.

'What a nice young man,' she remarked artlessly.

'He's not all that young, Mother...'

'Young for a professor, surely. Don't you like him, darling?'

'I hardly know him; he offered me a lift. I believe he's a very good surgeon in his own field.'

Mrs Blount studied her daughter's heightened colour. 'Tom will be home for half-term in a couple of weeks' time; I suppose you won't be able to come while he's here. George and Paul will be here too.'

'I'll do my best—Ida's just back from sick leave; she might not mind doing my weekend if I do hers on the following week. I'll see what she says and phone you.'

It was lovely being home; she helped her father with the small animals, drove him around to farms needing his help, and helped her mother around the house, catching up on the village gossip with Mrs Broom, who came twice a week to oblige. She was a small round woman who knew everyone's business and passed it on to anyone who would listen, but, since she wasn't malicious, no one minded. It didn't surprise Sophie in the least to hear that the professor had been seen, looked at closely and approved, although she had to squash Mrs

Broom's assumption that she and he had a romantic attachment.

'Oh, well,' said Mrs Broom, 'it's early days—you never know.' She added severely, 'Time you was married, Miss Sophie.'

The week passed quickly; the days weren't long enough and now that the evenings were closing in there were delightful hours to spend round the drawing-room fire, reading and talking and just sitting doing nothing at all. She missed the professor, not only his company but the fact that he was close by even though she might not see him for days on end. His suggestion of friendship, which she hadn't taken seriously, became something to be considered. But perhaps he hadn't been serious—hadn't he said 'Nothing serious'? She would, she decided, be a little cool when next they met.

He came just before eight o'clock on Sunday evening and all her plans to be cool were instantly wrecked. He got out of the car and when she opened the door and went to meet him, he flung a great arm around her shoulders and kissed her cheek, and that in full view of her mother and father. She had no chance to express her feelings about that, for his cheerful greeting overrode the indignant words she would have uttered. He was behaving like a family friend of long standing and at the same time combining it with beautiful manners; she could see that her parents were delighted with him.

This is the last time, reflected Sophie, going indoors again. All that nonsense about casual friends and needing male companionship; he's no better than a steamroller.

Anything less like that cumbersome machine would have been hard to imagine. The professor's manners were impeccable and after his unexpected embrace of her person he became the man she imagined him to be: rather quiet, making no attempt to draw attention to himself, and presently, over the coffee Mrs Blount offered, becoming engrossed in a conversation concerning the rearing of farm animals with his host. Sophie drank her coffee too hot and burnt her tongue and pretended to herself that she wasn't listening to his voice, deep and unhurried and somehow soothing. She didn't want to be soothed; she was annoyed.

It was the best part of an hour before the professor asked her if she was ready to leave; she bit back the tart reply that she had been ready ever since he had arrived and, with a murmur about putting Mabel into her basket, took herself out of the room. Five minutes later she reappeared, the imprisoned Mabel in one hand, her shoulder-bag swinging, kissed her parents, and, accompanied by the professor, now bearing the cat basket, went out to the car.

The professor wasn't a man to prolong goodbyes; she had time to wave to her mother and father standing in the porch before the Bentley slipped out of the drive and into the lane.

'Do I detect a coolness? What have I done? I could feel you seething for the last hour.'

'Kissing me like that,' said Sophie peevishly. 'Whatever next?' Before she could elaborate he said smoothly,

'But we are friends, are we not, Sophie? Besides, you looked pleased to see me.'

A truthful girl, she had to admit to that.

'There you are, then,' said the professor and eased a large well shod foot down so that the Bentley sped through the lanes and presently on to the main road.

'When do you have nights off?' he wanted to know.

'Oh, not until Tuesday and Wednesday of next week . . .'

'I'll take you out some time.'

'That would be very nice,' said Sophie cautiously, 'but don't you have to go back to Holland?'

'Not until the middle of next week. Let us make hay while the sun shines.'

'Your English is very good.'

'So it should be. I had—we all had—an English dragon for a nanny.'

'You have brothers and sisters?'

'Two brothers, five sisters.' He sent the Bentley smoothly round a slow-moving Ford driven by a man in a cloth cap. 'I am the eldest.'

'Like me,' said Sophie. 'What I mean is, like I.'

'We have much in common,' observed the professor. 'What a pity that I have to operate in the morning; we might have had lunch together.'

Sophie felt regret but she said nothing. The professor, she felt, was taking over far too rapidly; they hardly knew each other. She almost jumped out of her seat when he said placidly, 'We have got to get to know each other as quickly as possible.'

She said faintly, 'Oh, do we? Why?'

He didn't answer that but made some trivial remark about their surroundings. He was sometimes a tiresome man, reflected Sophie.

When they arrived at her lodgings he carried Mabel's
basket up to her room under the interested eye of Miss
Phipps, but he didn't go into it. His goodbye was casually
friendly and he said nothing about seeing her again. She
worried about that as she got ready for bed, but in the
chilly light of morning common sense prevailed. He was
just being polite, uttering one of those meaningless remarks which weren't supposed to be taken seriously.

She spent the morning cleaning her room, washing
her smalls and buying her household necessities from
the corner shop at the end of the street. In the afternoon
she washed her hair and did her nails, turned up the gas
fire until the room was really warm, made a pot of tea,
and sat with Mabel on her lap, reading a novel one of
her friends had lent her; but after the first few pages she
decided that it was boring her and turned to her own
thoughts instead. They didn't bore her at all, for they
were of the professor, only brought to an end when she
dozed off for a while. Then it was time to get ready to
go on duty, give Mabel a final hug and walk the short
distance to St Agnes's. It was a horrid evening, damp,
dark and chilly, and she hoped as she entered the hospital doors that it would be a quiet night.

It was a busy one; the day sister handed over thankfully, leaving two patients to be admitted and a short
line of damp and depressed people with septic fingers,
sprained ankles and minor cuts to be dealt with. Sophie
saw with satisfaction that she had Staff Nurse Pitt to
support her and three students, two of them quite senior,
the third a rather timid-looking girl. She'll faint if we
get anything really nasty in, thought Sophie, and handed
her over to the care of Jean Pitt, who was a motherly

soul with a vast patience. She did a swift round of the patients then, making sure that there was nothing that the casualty officer couldn't handle without the need of X-rays or further help. And, the row of small injuries dealt with and Tim Bailey, on duty for the first time, soothed with coffee and left in the office to write up his notes, she sent the nurses in turn to the little kitchen beside the office to have their own coffee. It was early yet and for the moment the place was empty.

Not for long, though; the real work of the night began then with the first of the ambulances; a street accident, a car crash, a small child fallen from an open window—they followed each other in quick succession. It was after two o'clock in the morning when Sophie paused long enough to gobble a sandwich and swallow a mug of coffee. Going to the midnight meal had been out of the question; she had been right about the most junior of the students, who had fainted as they cut the clothes off an elderly woman who had been mugged; she had been beaten and kicked and slashed with a knife, and Sophie, even though she saw such sights frequently, was full of sympathy for the girl; she had been put in one of the empty cubicles with a mug of tea and told to stay there until she felt better, but it had made one pair of hands less ...

She went off duty in a blur of tiredness, ate her breakfast without knowing what she was eating, and took herself off to her flatlet, and even Miss Phipps refrained from gossiping, but allowed her to mount the stairs in peace. Once there, it took no time at all to see to Mabel, have her bath and fall into bed.

That night set the pattern for her week. Usually there was a comparatively quiet night from time to time, but each night seemed busier than the last, and at the weekend, always worse than the weekdays, there was no respite, and even with the addition of a young male nurse to take over when one of the student nurses had nights off it was still back-breaking work. On Monday night, after a long session with a cardiac failure, Tim Bailey observed tiredly, 'I don't know how you stick it, Sophie, night after night...'

'I do sometimes wonder myself. But I've nights off—only two, though, because Ida isn't well again.'

'You'll go home?'

She nodded tiredly. 'It will be heaven, sleep and eat and then sleep and eat. What about you?'

'Two more nights, a couple of days off and back to day duty.' He put down his mug. 'And there's the ambulance again...'

Sophie ate her breakfast in a dream, but a happy one; she would go home just as soon as she could throw a few things into a bag and get Mabel into her basket. Lunch—eaten in the warmth of the kitchen—and then bed until suppertime and then bed again. She went out to the entrance in a happy daze, straight into the professor's waistcoat.

'You're still here?' she asked him owlishly. 'I thought you'd gone.'

'No, no.' He urged her into the Bentley. 'I'll drive you home, but first to your room.'

She was too tired to argue; ten minutes later she was in her flatlet, bundling things into her overnight bag, showering and dressing, not bothering with her face or

hair, and then hurrying down to the door again in case
he had changed his mind and gone. Her beautiful,
anxious face, bereft of make-up, had never looked love-
lier. The professor schooled his handsome features into
placid friendliness, stowed her into the car, settled Mabel
on the back seat, and drove away, not forgetting to wave
in a civil manner to Miss Phipps.

Sophie tossed her mane of hair, tied with a bit of
ribbon, over her shoulder. 'You're very kind,' she muttered. 'I hope I'm not taking you out of your way.' She
closed her eyes and slept peacefully for half an hour and
woke refreshed to find that they were well on the way
to her home.

She said belatedly, 'I told Mother I'd be home about
one o'clock.'

'I phoned. Don't fuss, Sophie.'

'Fuss? Fuss? I'm not—anyway, you come along and
change all my plans without so much as a by your leave...
I'm sorry, I'm truly sorry, I didn't mean a word of that;
I'm tired and so I say silly things. I'm so grateful.'

When he didn't answer she said, 'Really I am—don't
be annoyed...'

'When you know me better, Sophie, you will know
that I seldom get annoyed—angry, impatient...cer-
tainly, but I think never any of these with you.' He gave
her a brief smile. 'Why have you only two nights off
after such a gruelling eight nights?'

'The other night sister—Ida Symonds—is ill again.'

'There is no one to take her place?'

'Not for the moment. The junior night sister on the
surgical wards is taking over while I'm away.'

They were almost there when he said casually, 'I'm going back to Holland tomorrow.'

'Not for good?'

Her voice was sharp, and he asked lightly, 'Will you miss me? I hope so.'

She stared out at the wintry countryside. 'Yes.'

'We haven't had that lunch yet, have we? Perhaps we can arrange that when I come again.'

'Will you be back soon?'

'Oh, yes. I have to go to Birmingham and then Leeds and then on to Edinburgh.'

'But not here, in London?'

'Probably.' He sounded vague and she decided that he was just being civil again.

'I expect you'll be glad to be home again?'

'Yes.' He didn't add anything to that, and a few moments later they had reached her home and were greeted by her mother at the door before the car had even stopped, smiling a warm welcome. Not a very satisfactory conversation, reflected Sophie, in fact hardly a conversation at all. She swiftly returned her mother's hug and went indoors with the professor and Mabel's basket hard on her heels. He put the basket down, unbuttoned her coat, took it off, tossed it on to a chair and followed it with his own, and then gave her a gentle shove towards the warmth of the kitchen. Montgomery and Mercury had come to meet them and he let Mabel out of her basket to join them as Mrs Blount set the coffee on the table.

'Will you stay for lunch?' she asked hopefully.

'I would have liked that, but I've still some work to clear up before I return to Holland.'

'You'll be back?' He hid a smile at the look of disappointment on her face.

'Oh, yes, quite soon, I hope.' He glanced at Sophie. 'Sophie is tired out. I won't stay for long, for I'm sure she is longing for her bed.'

He was as good as his word, saying all the right things to his hostess, with the hope that he would see her again before very long, and then bidding Sophie goodbye with the advice that she should sleep the clock round if possible and then get out in the fresh air. 'We are sure to meet when I get back to England,' he observed, and she murmured politely. He hadn't said how long that would be, she thought peevishly, and he need not think that she was at his beck and call every time he felt like her company. She was, of course, overlooking the fact that her company had been a poor thing that morning and if he had expected anything different he must have been very disappointed. All the same, she saw him go with regret.

The two days went in a flash, a comforting medley of eating, sleeping and pottering in the large, rather untidy garden, tying things up, digging things out of the ground before it became hard with frost, and cutting back the roses. By the time she had to return to the hospital she was her old self again, and her mother, looking at her lovely face, wished that the professor had been there to see her daughter. She comforted herself with the thought that he had said that he would be back and it seemed to her that he was a man whose word could be relied on. He and Sophie were only friends at the moment, but given time and opportunity... She sighed. She didn't want her Sophie to be hurt as she had been hurt all those years ago.

It was November now, casting a gloom over the shabby streets around the hospital. Even on a bright summer's day they weren't much to look at; now they were depressing, littered with empty cans of Coca Cola, fish and chip papers and the more lurid pages of the tabloid Press. Sophie, picking her way towards her own front door a few hours before she was due on duty again, thought of the street cleaners who so patiently swept and tidied only to have the same rubbish waiting for them next time they came around. Rather like us, I suppose, she reflected. We get rid of one lot of patients and there's the next lot waiting.

Miss Phipps was hovering as she started up the stairs. 'Had a nice little holiday?' she wanted to know. 'Came back by train, did you?'

Sophie said that yes, she had, and if she didn't hurry she would be late for work, which wasn't quite true, but got her safely up the rest of the stairs and to her room, where she released Mabel, fed her, made herself a cup of tea, and loaded her shoulder-bag with everything she might need during the night. She seldom had the chance to open it, but it was nice to think that everything was there.

The accident room was quiet when she went on duty, but Casualty was still teeming with patients. She took over from the day sister, ran her eye down the list of patients already seen, checked with her Staff and phoned for Tim Bailey to come as soon as possible and cast his eye over what she suspected was a Pott's fracture, and began on the task of applying dressings to the patients who needed them.

Tim arrived five minutes later. 'I've seen this lot,' he said snappily. 'They only need dressings and injections; surely you——?'

'Yes, I know and of course we'll see to those... This man's just come in—I think he's a Pott's, and if you say so I'll get him to X-Ray if you'd like to sign the form.'

She gave him a charming smile and she had sounded almost motherly, so that he laughed. 'Sorry—I didn't mean to snap. Let's look at this chap.'

She had been right; he signed the form and told her, 'Give me a ring and I'll put on a plaster, but give me time to eat my dinner, will you?'

'You'll have time for two dinners by the time I've got hold of X-Ray; it's Miss Short and she is always as cross as two sticks.'

The man with the Pott's fracture was followed by more broken bones, a stab wound and a crushed hand; a normal night, reflected Sophie, going sleepily to her bed, and so were the ensuing nights, including the usual Saturday night's spate of street fights and road accidents. The following week bid fair to be the same, so that by the time she was due for nights off again she was more than a little tired. All the same, she thought as she coaxed Mabel into her basket and started on her journey home, it would have been nice to find the professor waiting for her outside the door.

Wishful thinking; there was no sign of him.

CHAPTER THREE

HOME for Sophie was bliss after the cold greyness of the East End. The quiet countryside, bare now that it was almost winter, was a much needed change from the crowded streets around the hospital. She spent her days visiting the surrounding farms with her father and pottering around the house, and her nights in undisturbed sleep. She was happy—though perhaps not perfectly happy, for the professor had a bothersome way of intruding into her thoughts, and none of the sensible reasons for forgetting him seemed adequate. If she had been given an opportunity she would have talked about him to her mother, but that lady never mentioned him.

She went back to the hospital half hoping that she would see him—not that she wished to particularly, she reminded herself, but he had said that he would return...

There was no news of him, although there was plenty of gossip around the breakfast-table after her first night's duty, most of it wild guessing and Gill's half-serious plans as to what she would do and say when she next saw him. 'For I'll be the lucky one, won't I?' She grinned round the table. 'If he's operating I can always think up a good reason for being in Theatre during the day...' There was a burst of laughter at this and she added, 'You may well laugh, but I'll be the first one to see him.'

As it turned out, she was wrong.

Sophie, bent on keeping a young man with terrible head injuries alive, working desperately at it, obeying Tim's quick instructions with all the skill she could muster, stood a little on one side to allow the surgical registrar to reach the patient, and at the same time realised that there was someone with him. She knew who it was even before she saw him, and although her heart gave a joyful little leap she didn't let it interfere with her work. He came from behind and bent his height to examine the poor crushed head, echoing Peter Small's cheerful 'Hello, Sophie' with a staid 'Good evening, Sister'.

She muttered a reply, intent on what she was doing, and for the next half an hour was far too busy to give him a thought, listening to the two men and doing as she was bid, taking blood for cross-matching, summoning X-ray and the portable machine, and warning Theatre that the professor would be operating within the hour. She heard Gill's delighted chuckle when she told her.

At breakfast Gill gave everyone a blow-by-blow account of the professor's activities. He had done a marvellous bit of surgery, she assured them, and afterwards he had had a mug of tea in her office. 'He was rather quiet,' she explained, 'but he had only been here for a couple of hours, discussing some cases with Peter; he must have been tired...' She brightened. 'There are sure to be some more cases during the night,' she added pensively. 'I've got nights off in two days' time. He's on the theatre list to do two brain tumours tomorrow; probably he'll be free after that.'

She called across the table, 'Hey, Sophie, didn't he go to the accident room? Did he say anything to you?'

'He said, "Good evening, Sister", and asked me where the man came from.'

Gill said happily, not meaning to be unkind, 'I dare say he likes small, fragile-looking girls like me.'

They got up to go then and Sophie changed out of her uniform and made for the entrance. It was raining again, which was probably why she felt depressed.

The professor was lounging against a wall, studying the notice-board. He straightened up when he saw her and walked towards her. When he was near enough he said, 'Hello, Sophie,' and smiled. It was a smile to warm her, and she smiled back from a tired unmade-up face.

'I'm glad you were there,' she said. 'Will he do?'

'I believe so—it's early days yet, but he's got a chance.' He fell in beside her, walking to the door. 'Are you glad because I was there to deal with the patient or were you glad to see me, Sophie?'

She stopped to look at him. 'Both.'

He tucked a hand under her elbow. 'Good, still friends? I'm not operating until this afternoon and we both need some fresh air. Come along.'

She was whizzed through the door, by no means willingly. 'I have no wish for fresh air,' she told him, peevish after a long night's work. 'I'm going to bed.'

'Well, of course you are, but not just yet. We'll go to Epping Forest, have a brisk walk and a cup of coffee, and be back here by midday.'

'Mabel,' said Sophie feebly.

'We'll go there first. I shall come up with you, otherwise you might forget me and go to sleep.'

'No, no. You mustn't come up. I won't be more than five minutes or so.'

He stuffed her into the car and got in beside her and a few minutes later got out to open her door and usher her across the pavement and in through the shabby front door. 'Five minutes,' he reminded her and turned to engage in conversation with Miss Phipps, who had darted out, her wig askew, intent on a chat.

Mabel's wants attended to, her face made up after a fashion and her hair tidied, Sophie went back downstairs and was forced to admire the way in which the professor drew his conversation with her landlady to its conclusion in such a way that the lady was under the impression that it was she who had brought it to a close.

'Anyone would think that you liked her,' said Sophie waspishly. She wished suddenly that she hadn't come; thinking about it, she couldn't remember saying that she would in the first place.

'No, no, nothing of the sort, but if she should take a dislike to me she might show me the door, and then we would have to meet in the street or a park—all very well in the summer, but this is no weather for dallying around the East End.'

Sophie drew a deep breath. 'What do you mean—"have to meet"? We don't have to do anything of the sort.'

'My dear girl, use your tired wits. How are we to get to know each other unless we spend time in each other's company?'

'Why do we have to get to know each other? You don't even live here.'

She realised what a silly remark that was as soon as it was uttered.

'A powerful argument for our frequent meetings when I am,' he told her placidly. 'You have been home since I saw you last?'

His gentle conversation soothed her. She was tired but no longer edgy and by the time they reached the comparative quiet of the forest she was ready enough to walk its paths with him. Indeed, when presently he suggested that they should go in search of coffee she felt reluctant to leave, not sure whether it was the peace and quiet around them or his company which she was loath to give up.

They had been in the car five minutes or so when she pointed out that he had left the road back.

He reassured her. 'I thought we might have our coffee at Ingatestone; there's rather a nice place on the Roman Road.'

The nice place was a fifteenth-century hotel, quite beautifully restored. It would be busy in the evenings, she judged, but now there were few people there. They sat in a lovely room by a pleasant fire and drank their coffee, but Sophie wasn't allowed to stay for long. 'If we sit here much longer,' observed the professor, 'you'll fall asleep and I shall be forced to carry you upstairs to that room of yours, and all my efforts to keep Miss Phipps sweet would be useless.'

Sophie, warm and content, laughed at that.

Back once more, he saw her very correctly to the front door, bade her a brief goodbye, and drove away, leaving Sophie to fend off Miss Phipps's curiosity with the observation that she was almost too sleepy to get to her room...

She didn't see him during the next night. For once it was fairly quiet and all the night sisters were in the canteen at the same time for their midnight meal. It was Gill who mentioned him first. 'He operated at one o'clock,' she grumbled. 'I simply couldn't get up in the middle of the day, and besides, I couldn't think of a good excuse to turn up in Theatre. But luck is on my side, girls; he's operating at half-past eight this morning, so I shall forget something and go back to Theatre and chat him up.'

'I must say, you're keen,' said someone. 'Don't any of us get a look-in?'

Gill beamed round the table. 'Let's face it, I'm just his type; big men like little women.'

Sophie, her mouth full of scrambled egg, said nothing.

She saw the Bentley parked in the consultant's parking space as she left the hospital. He would be operating by now and doubtless Gill had found an excuse to go back to Theatre on some pretext or other. It was probably true, reflected Sophie, walking back to her flatlet in the teeth of a nasty little wind, that big men liked small girls. If so, why did he bother to see her? To go to the trouble of meeting her mother and father, take her for brisk walks for her health's sake? She pondered the problem and she couldn't find an answer. A conceited girl might have concluded that it was her strikingly pretty person which attracted him, but she wasn't conceited; three brothers had seen to that. She bade Miss Phipps an absent-minded good morning and gained the solitude of her room to find Mabel waiting for her with impatience.

She fed her, had a bath, made herself a mug of cocoa, and went to bed trying not to think how pleasant a brisk walk in Epping Forest would have been. Tomorrow, she told herself sleepily, she would take a bus and tramp round Hyde Park even if it poured with rain. She closed her eyes and, lulled by Mabel's gentle purr, she slept.

A disgruntled Gill told her as they sat at their midnight meal that although she had gone back to the theatre with some excuse the professor had already started to operate and hadn't finished until the early afternoon. 'And on top of that,' she went on, 'he's gone to France— a last-chance op on a little girl with a brain tumour. There are several more cases lined up for him here, so he's bound to come back.' Her blue eyes were screwed up with annoyance. 'I wish I were on day duty. On the other hand, I'd see more of him at night.'

'Only if some poor unfortunate came in with severe head injuries, and who would want that?' Sophie had spoken tartly, and Gill gave her a searching look.

'Well, no, of course not. Sophie, I do believe that you haven't a spark of romance in you. If you weren't so large yourself you'd have the men falling about to get at you.'

There was a burst of laughter; 'large' hardly described Sophie's magnificent shape, and several voices pointed this out, while she, unperturbed, spooned her milk pudding, aware that a gratifying number of men had proposed to her and professed themselves in love with her. She had liked them all, but not enough to marry them—the only one she had felt differently about was a dim memory now, and she wasn't sure if she believed in love any more... Her thoughts were interrupted by

her bleep and she sped away to deal with a very drunk
man who had fallen through a glass door. His injuries
weren't serious but needed a good deal of stitching, and
it took some time to get his address and get his wife to
come and fetch him home. It was the worst hour of the
long night by now—almost four o'clock, when the desire
to sleep was strong, to be countered by cups of tea and
the hopeful tidying-up of the accident room and
Casualty, although Sophie couldn't remember a morning
when there hadn't been at least two patients arriving just
as everything was pristine and ready for the day staff.

True to the promise she had made herself, she spent
an hour in Hyde Park that morning, walking at a good
pace and actually rather enjoying it. The weather had
improved too and the air there was fresh, and the
Serpentine gave an illusion of the country. She took a
bus back to her lodgings, made her cocoa, had a bath,
and fell into bed to sleep at once and not wake until
Mabel, impatient for her food, roused her with an urgent
paw.

Three more days, thought Sophie, diving into her
clothes while the kettle boiled, and it's nights off again.

The night ahead of her, did she but know it, was going
to be a very busy one, and at the end of it she was too
tired to eat her breakfast; she pushed cornflakes round
her plate, drank several cups of tea, and got up from
the table.

'You've had a busy night,' observed the men's medical
ward sister, who hadn't. 'You must be dying for
your bed.'

'It was rather much—luckily it isn't like that every night. There was this rally about something or other, and they always end up in a fight...'

'Nights off soon?' asked someone.

'Three more nights, and I've been promised a male student nurse; as long as Ida doesn't go off sick again, the future looks rosy. Bye for now.'

She went along to change, flinging her clothes on anyhow, something she would never dream of doing normally, but now all she wanted was her bed.

The professor was just outside the door as she went through it. He took her arm and marched her across the forecourt, opened the Bentley's door, and urged her inside. Only when they were sitting side by side did he say, 'Good morning, Sophie, only I see that it isn't for you. You've had a bad night?'

She found her voice, indignant but squeaky with tiredness. 'Yes, and if you don't mind I want to go home and go to bed—now.' She added as an afterthought, 'Good morning, Professor.'

'So you shall. Did you eat your breakfast?'

'I'm not hungry.' As she spoke she was aware that if she went to bed without a meal she would wake after an hour or two and not sleep again, but that, she considered, was her business.

The professor edged the car out into the street. 'First we will see to Mabel, then we will go together and have breakfast, and then you shall go to bed.'

'I don't want——' began Sophie.

'No, of course you don't, but just be a good girl and do as I say.' He had stopped before her door and was already helping her out. 'I'm coming up with you.'

She stood where she was. 'Indeed you're not. Miss
Phipps——'

'Sophie, I beg you to stop fussing; just leave everything to me.'

He opened the street door and pushed her ahead of
him. 'Go on up,' he told her and turned to Miss Phipps,
already with her head round the door.

Sophie did as she was told, vaguely listening to his
deep voice. He sounded serious and she could hear Miss
Phipps making sympathetic noises. She wondered what
he had said to earn that lady's concern as she unlocked
her own door, flung her bag on the divan, and went to
get Mabel's breakfast. She was spooning the cat food
into a saucer when the professor knocked and came in.
The room was cold and he lit the gas fire, took the tin
from her to finish the job, and told her to wash her face
and comb her hair. 'And no hanging about, I beg you;
I'm famished.'

She paused with a towel over her arm on the way to
the bathroom. 'Don't they give you breakfast at St
Agnes's?'

'Oh, yes, if I asked for it. I came over on a night ferry
and came straight to the hospital.'

'An emergency?'

'If you are an emergency, then yes. Go and wash your
face, Sophie.'

She went through the door and then poked her head
back round it. 'Haven't you been to bed?'

'No, I drove down to Calais.'

Her dark eyes, huge with a lack of sleep, stared across
the room at him. 'But why...?' she began, only to be

told at once to do something to her face. 'For I refuse
to take you out looking "like patience on a monument".

'"Smiling at grief",' muttered Sophie, hurrying down
the stairs.

She returned five minutes later, her face washed and
made-up after a fashion. She had brushed her hair too
so that it was tidy in front, although the coil at the back
was in need of attention.

'Take the pins out and tie it back,' sighed the professor, which she did, finding a bit of ribbon in her work
basket and making a neat bow.

He settled Mabel in her basket, switched off the fire
and opened the door. 'You shouldn't hide your hair,' he
said as she went past him.

She looked at him in astonishment. 'I couldn't possibly
go on duty with it hanging down my back.'

He only smiled down at her, and, for some reason,
feeling awkward, she added, 'I don't always bother to
put it up when I'm at home.'

'Oh, good,' said the professor, pressing his vast person
against the wall so that she might pass him.

He whisked her past Miss Phipps with a brief, 'We
shall be back presently, Miss Phipps,' before that lady
could so much as open her mouth, and gently bundled
Sophie into the car. Catching her breath as he drove
away, she asked, 'Where are we going?'

'To my house to eat breakfast; it should be ready and
waiting for us.'

'Your house? I thought you lived in Holland...'

'I do.' He didn't offer any more information and
somehow she didn't like to ask and sat silent while he
drove across the city, but as he threaded his way through

the one-way streets in the West End she ventured, 'You live in London?'

He turned the car into one of the narrow fashionable streets of Belgravia. 'Oh, yes.' He slowed the car and stopped before a terrace of Regency houses. 'Here we are.'

The houses were tall and narrow with bay windows and important doors gleaming with paint and highly polished doorknockers. He urged her across the narrow pavement, fished out a bunch of keys, and opened his door.

The hall was long and narrow, and as they went in a man came to meet them.

'Mornin', guv,' he said cheerfully. 'There's a nice bit of breakfast all ready for you and the lady.'

He was youngish, with nondescript hair and a round face in which a pair of small blue eyes twinkled, and he was most decidedly a Cockney.

The professor returned his greeting affably. 'This is Percy, who runs the place for me together with Mrs Wiffen. This is Miss Blount, as famished as I am.'

'Okey-doke, guv, leave it to me. Pleased to meet you, miss, I'm sure.'

His little eyes surveyed her and he smiled. 'You go right to the table and I'll bring in the food.'

He took Sophie's coat and opened a door. 'Gotta lotta post, guv,' he observed. 'It's in yer study.'

The professor thanked him. 'Later, Percy—let me know if there are any phone calls.'

The room they entered was at the front of the house, not over-large but furnished with great taste, its mulberry-red walls contrasting with the maple-wood furniture. The table was circular, decked with a white damask cloth, with shining silver and blue and white china, and the coffee-pot Percy was setting on the table was silver, very plain save for a coat of arms on one side. Sophie took the seat offered by the professor and cast a quick look round her. She came from a family in comfortable circumstances, but this was more than comfort, it was luxury, albeit understated. There was a bracket clock on the mantelpiece which she was sure was eighteenth-century, perhaps earlier; it suited the room exactly, so did the draped brocade curtains at the bow window and the fine carpet, almost threadbare with age, on the floor. The professor interrupted her inspection.

'Pour the coffee, will you, Sophie? Do you want to talk about your night or shall we lay plans for our next meeting?'

A remark which rather took her breath. She had it back by the time Percy had served them with a splendid breakfast and then gone away again. 'Are we going to meet again?'

He handed her the toast rack. 'Of course we are; what a silly remark. When do you have your nights off?'

'I have three more nights to work.'

'Good. I'll drive you home, but shall we see if we can spend a little time together first? Could you manage to spend the afternoon with me before we go? Go to bed for a few hours and I'll fetch you about one o'clock; we can have lunch somewhere and walk for a while.'

She speared a mushroom and ate it thoughtfully. She was feeling quite wide awake now and eyed him uncertainly. 'Well, yes, I could, but why?'

'Because some exercise will do you good and Epping Forest is on our way to your home.' Which didn't really answer her question.

She crunched a morsel of perfectly cooked bacon. 'Well, all right. It's very kind of you. I'd like to be home by suppertime, though.' She paused, looking at him. 'Perhaps you would like to have supper with us before you drive back here?'

'That,' said the professor gravely, 'would be most kind if your mother has no objection.'

'No. She'll be delighted. She likes you,' said Sophie matter-of-factly, not seeing the gleam in her companion's eyes. She applied herself to her breakfast with unselfconscious pleasure while they talked about nothing much, undemanding chat which was very soothing. It was a lovely house, she thought, welcoming and warm—one could live very happily in it...

She could have lingered there, uncaring of sleep, but the silvery chimes of the clock reminded her of her bed and she glanced at the professor, who nodded his handsome head just as though she had spoken.

'I'm going to take you back now,' he told her. 'Go to bed and sleep, Sophie, ready for another night.'

Percy came then to help her with her coat, and she thanked him for her breakfast. 'I hope it didn't give you too much extra work.'

'Lor' no, miss. Nice ter 'ave a bit of company. Me and Mrs Wiffen and the cat get lonely when the guv's away.'

In the car she asked, 'Why does Percy call you guv? I mean, it's a bit unusual, isn't it? He's the houseman or valet or something, isn't he?'

'Ah, but Percy is unusual. I removed a tumour from his brain some five years ago and at the time he said that he would look after my interests until either he or I should die. I took him at his word and he is splendid at his job and always cheerful. As far as I'm concerned, he may call me what he likes. Did you like him?'

'Yes—I imagine you could trust him completely.'

'Indeed I do. There isn't much he can't do or arrange even at a moment's notice. I can go to and from Holland knowing that he will look after things for me.'

He had stopped the car outside Miss Phipps's house, and for a moment Sophie compared it with the house they had just left. A foolish thing to do, she reminded herself bracingly, and got out as the professor opened the door for her. Nothing could have been brisker than his manner as he saw her to the door and bade her goodbye.

'I suppose that was his good deed for the day,' said Sophie to an inattentive Mabel.

During the next three nights she heard a good deal about the professor. He was operating each day and Gill reported faithfully what he did and said to her and what she had said to him and thought about later; none of it amounted to much. There was no sign of him, though, and she went home to the flat at the end of her last night's duty feeling uncertain. True, he had said that he would drive her home, true also that he was calling for her at one o'clock and taking her out to lunch, but supposing he had forgotten or, worse, had issued a vague invitation, not meaning a word of it?

Common sense told her that that was unlikely; she went to bed as soon as she got to her room, with rather a nice tweed skirt and needlecord jacket with a washed-silk blouse to go under it lying ready to get into when she got up.

She set her alarm for half-past twelve, got up rather reluctantly, dressed, and, with her face nicely made-up and her hair in its smooth, intricate coils, urged Mabel into her basket, swung her shoulder-bag over her arm, and went downstairs.

The Bentley was outside with the professor at the wheel, reading a newspaper. He got out as she opened the door, dealt with the bag and Mabel, and settled her beside him.

'Lunch first?' he asked. 'I've booked a table at that place at Ingatestone.'

They talked in a desultory fashion as he drove, pleasant talk which required no effort on her part, and over their lunch he kept their conversation easygoing and rambling, not touching on any topic that was personal. Sophie, refreshed by her short sleep, agreed readily to a dish of hors-d'oeuvres, grilled Dover sole and sherry trifle and enjoyed them with an appetite somewhat sharpened by a week or more of solid hospital cooking and snatched sandwiches.

'That was delicious,' she observed, pouring their coffee.

'Splendid. We have time for an hour's walk before we need drive on to your home.'

A short drive brought them to Epping Forest. He parked the car and they started along one of the well marked paths running between the trees and dense shrubbery, almost leafless now, quiet and sheltered, winding away out of sight. Presently they came to a small clearing with an old crumbling wall overlooking a stretch of open country, and by common consent paused to lean against it and admire the view. The professor said quietly, 'May I take it that we are now good, firm friends, Sophie?'

She had had a sleep and a delicious lunch and the quiet trees around her were soothing. She smiled up at him; he was safe and solid and a good companion. 'Oh, yes.'

'Then perhaps you know what I am going to say next. Will you marry me, Sophie?'

Her smile melted into a look of utter surprise. 'Marry you? Why? Whatever for?'

He smiled at that. 'We are good friends; have we not just agreed about that? We enjoy doing the same things, laughing at the same things... I want someone to share my life, Sophie, a companion, someone to make my house a home, someone to be friends with my friends.'

She met his intent look honestly, although her cheeks were pink. 'But we don't—that is, shouldn't there be love as well?'

'Have you ever been in love, Sophie?' He wasn't looking at her now, but at the view before them.

She took a long time to answer, but he showed no impatience. Presently she said, 'Yes, I have. Oh, it was years ago; I was nineteen and I loved him so much. He threw me over for an older woman, a young widow. She was small and pretty and beautifully dressed and had money; I felt like a clumsy beanpole beside her. I would have given anything to have been five feet tall and slim... It's funny, but I can't remember what he looked like any more, but I'll never forget how I felt. I never want to feel like that again—it was like the end of the world.'

He still didn't look at her, but he flung a great arm across her shoulders and she felt comforted by it.

'You never think of him?'

'No. No, not for a long time now. It wasn't love—the kind of love that swallows up everything else—was it?'

'One is very vulnerable at nineteen, and had you thought that, if you had married this man on a flood of infatuation, by now, eight years later, you would be bitterly regretting it? One changes, you know.'

She turned to look at him. It wasn't just his good looks; he was so sure about things, so dependable and, underneath his rather austere manner, very kind.

'You haven't answered my question.'

'You answered it yourself, didn't you? You were hurt badly once; for that to happen a second time is something you will never allow. My dear, marriage isn't all a matter of falling in love and living happily ever after. Liking is as important as loving in its way; feeling comfortable with each other is important too—and friendship. Add these things up and you have the kind of love which makes a happy marriage.'

'What about Romeo and Juliet, or Abelard and Héloïse? They loved——'

'Ah—that is something which only a few people are fortunate enough to share.'

His arm was still around her, but he made no attempt to draw her closer. 'I think that we may be happy together, Sophie. We do not know each other very well yet, but we have so little opportunity to meet. Would you consider marrying me and getting to know me after?

I am quite sure that we can be happy; but let us take our time learning about each other, gaining each other's affection. We will live as friends if you like until we are used to the idea of being man and wife; I'll not hurry you...'

'I don't know where you live—do you have parents?'

'Oh, yes. My father's a retired surgeon; he and my mother live in Friesland. I live there too; so do two of my sisters. The other three live in den Haag.'

'All in one house?' The idea appalled her.

He laughed. 'No, no. We all have homes of our own. Have you any leave due, Sophie?'

'A week, that's all.'

'Long enough. Can you manage to get free by the end of next week? I've nothing over here after that; I'll take you to Holland and you can make up your mind then.'

'I'm not sure, but I think this is a very funny kind of proposal,' said Sophie.

'Is it? I've not proposed marriage before, so I'm not qualified to give an opinion. Shall I start again and you tell me what to say?'

She laughed then and said, 'Don't be ridiculous,' and saw that he was smiling too, but she didn't see the gleam in his eye.

'I don't think that I can get a week off at such short notice,' Sophie said regretfully.

'Perhaps if I had a word... Apply to whoever it is who deals with such things when you get back on duty and see what happens.'

'All right, but I'm not certain...'

He said in a soothing voice, 'No, no, of course you're not. You would prefer to say nothing, I expect, for the time being.'

'Perhaps not at all,' said Sophie soberly.

'That seems to be a splendid idea.' He was all of a sudden brisk. 'Shall we go back to the car? Your mother doesn't expect us before the early evening, does she? Then let us find somewhere where we can have tea.'

It was obvious after a while that he wasn't going to refer to the matter again; she would dearly have liked to question him about his home in Holland, but she wasn't sure how to set about it. She liked him—there was no question about that—but she sensed that penetrating his reserve was something best left until she knew more about him. Sitting beside him as he drove away from the woods, she reflected that the idea of marrying him was beginning to take firm root in her head, which, considering she had never addressed him as other than professor or sir, seemed absurd.

CHAPTER FOUR

SOPHIE and the professor stopped at the Post House in Epping for their tea and, over buttered muffins and several cups of that reviving beverage, discussed everything under the sun but themselves. Sophie, ever hopeful, made several efforts to talk about her companion's life, but it was of no use; he gave her no encouragement at all. She gave up presently, feeling annoyed and trying not to show it, suspecting that he knew that and was secretly amused.

Her mother and father welcomed them with carefully restrained curiosity; the professor was becoming a fairly frequent visitor and, naturally enough, they were beginning to wonder why. It was after a leisurely supper, sitting in the comfortable drawing-room round the log fire, that he enlightened them.

'I am going back to Holland tomorrow for two days,' he told them in his calm, unhurried way, 'but I hope that I will see you again shortly.' He looked at Sophie. 'You won't mind, my dear, if I tell your parents that I have asked you to marry me?'

It was too late to say that yes, she did mind, anyway. Not that she did; she had been wondering all the evening what exactly she should say to her mother and father. Before they could say anything he went on, 'I shall be here for a week or so, which will give her time to decide if she will marry me or not. If she agrees, then I hope to take her to Holland with me so that she may meet my family and see my home. If she should refuse me I hope that she and I will remain friends and that I shall see you from time to time.'

Sophie found three pairs of eyes looking at her. 'I thought I'd like to think about it,' she said a little breathlessly. 'Just to be sure, you know.'

Her father said, 'Sensible girl,' and her mother observed,

'I would be delighted to see the pair of you married, but Sophie's quite right to think it over; love is for a lifetime.' She nodded her head in satisfaction. 'You're well suited,' she added.

They were content to leave it at that; the talk was of his journey the next day, Sophie's busy week and the various countries he visited from time to time, and presently he took his leave, and Sophie, feeling that it was expected of her, went with him to the door.

'When will you be back in England?' asked Sophie, once they were in the hall.

'In three days' time. I have to give a series of lectures.' He was standing close to her, but not touching her. 'Will you give me your answer then?'

She looked up into his face. He was smiling a little, friendly and relaxed and most reassuringly calm. 'I shall miss you.'

'And I you—that augurs well for our future, does it not?'

She said hesitantly, 'Well, yes, I suppose it does. I'll—I'll tell you when I see you.'

He bent his head and kissed her, a brief, comforting kiss, before he opened the door and got into his car, and drove away without looking back.

Tom, home from school while Sophie had nights off, declared himself delighted with the idea of her getting married. 'Splendid,' he crowed. 'Now I'll have somewhere to go for my holidays——'

'Don't count your chickens,' said Sophie severely. 'I haven't said I want to marry yet; we're not even engaged.'

'He's a prime fellow, Sophie, and he's got a Bentley.'

'Which is no reason for marrying anyone,' said Sophie firmly.

What would the reasons be if she did marry him? she wondered. He had been quite right; they got on well together and they liked each other. Liking someone that you were going to live with for the rest of your life was important. She would be a suitable wife to him too, since, being a nurse, she understood the kind of life he led and would make allowances for it. She wasn't a young girl either; she would be prepared to take over the duties of his household and cope with any special social life that he might have. She could see that from his point of view she was eminently suitable.

The thought depressed her, while at the same time she acknowledged his good sense in seeking a wife to suit his lifestyle. As for herself, she had no wish to fall in love again, with the chance of breaking her heart for the second time. On second thoughts, she acknowledged to herself that her heart couldn't have been broken, otherwise she wouldn't be considering the idea of marrying the professor. Rijk—she must remember to call him that.

Her parents had made no attempt to advise her, although they made it plain that they liked the professor; they also made it plain that she was old enough to make up her own mind, and George and Paul, when appraised of the situation, had given their opinions over the phone that he sounded a decent chap, and wasn't it about time she married anyway?

Sophie went back to St Agnes's with her mind very nearly, but not quite, made up, which was a good thing, because several busy nights in a row made it difficult for her to think of anything but her work and her bed.

Three days went by and there was no sign of the professor. There was no reason, she thought peevishly, why he couldn't have sent her a note at least, and surely he could have phoned her? She flounced out of the hospital with a cross, tired face, although she still managed to look beautiful.

The Bentley came smoothly into the forecourt as she crossed over, and the professor parked neatly and got out and strolled towards her.

His 'Good morning, Sophie' was cheerful, but she saw that he was tired.

She asked suspiciously, 'Have you just got here?' and then, remembering her manners, she said, 'Good morning, Rijk.'

'That is a most convenient ferry from Calais; even with delays on the motorway it still allows me time to reach you before you go to bed.'

He had a hand on her shoulder, urging her back to the car. 'We will go and attend to Mabel and then we will breakfast together.'

'Yes, well—all right.' She got into the car with the pleasant feeling that she wouldn't need to bother about anything any more. Common sense warned her that this was a piece of nonsense, but she was too tired to argue with herself. She asked, 'Have you been to bed?'

'No.' He smiled suddenly at her, and all the tired lines vanished. 'I had too much to think about.'

He stopped outside Miss Phipps's house and got out to open her door. 'Ten minutes? I don't feel up to your landlady; I'll wait here.'

'I'll be quick...'

It was a chilly morning and Mabel most obligingly wasted no time on the tiny balcony but nipped back smartly to eat her breakfast.

'I'll be back quite soon,' Sophie promised. Without bothering to do anything to her face or hair, she hurried back to the car.

The professor was asleep, his face as calm and placid as a child's, and she went round the bonnet and stealthily opened her door. Without opening his eyes he said, 'You have been quick,' and was all at once alert and wide awake.

'I didn't mean to wake you,' said Sophie. 'Are you sure you wouldn't like to go to your house and go straight to bed?'

'We are going straight to my house. As for bed, that will come later. Breakfast first.'

Percy flung the door wide as they got out of the car and greeted them with a cheerful, 'Morning, guv, morning, miss. Mrs Wiffen's got a smashing breakfast laid on. 'Ad a good trip, 'ave you?'

The professor replied that indeed he had and took Sophie's coat and tossed it to Percy, who caught it and hung it tidily away in the hall closet.

'There's a pile of letters in the study, but you'll eat first, eh?'

'Yes, thank you, Percy. As soon as you can get the breakfast on the table.'

'Watch me,' said Percy, and whizzed away as the professor urged Sophie into the dining-room.

There was a bright fire burning and the table was laid invitingly with patterned china, gleaming silver and a blue bowl of oranges as its centre-piece. As they sat down Percy came in with a tray, coffee and tea and covered silver dishes which he arranged on the sideboard, and then made a second journey with the toast rack.

'Thank you, Percy,' said the professor. 'We'll ring if we want anything.' He got up to serve Sophie. 'Bacon? Eggs? A mushroom or two? A grilled tomato?'

Sophie, her mouth watering, said yes to everything, and, feeling that she should do her share, asked, 'Coffee or tea?'

'Coffee, please...'

She poured tea for herself and they sat in companionable silence, eating the good food, but when Percy appeared to take away their plates and bring fresh toast the professor said, 'Not too tired to talk?'

Sophie piled butter and marmalade on to a corner of toast. 'No, that was a lovely breakfast, thank you very much.'

He sat back in his chair, his eyes on her face. 'And are we to share our breakfasts together, Sophie? You have had several days in which to decide. Bear in mind that I am impatient and like my own way, bad-tempered at times, too, although I have learnt to control it...'

'Are you trying to put me off?' asked Sophie. 'If you are it's too late, because I think I'd like to marry you.' She added diffidently, 'That's if you haven't changed your mind?'

He smiled at her across the table. 'No, Sophie, I made up my mind to marry you when I first saw you standing there in the middle of the pavement...'

She opened her eyes at that. 'You did? How could you possibly decide something like that so quickly?'

'I realised that I had at last found a girl who matched me in height and so I decided to snap you up.'

She looked at him uncertainly. 'You're joking, aren't you?'

He didn't answer, but got up and went and pulled her gently from her chair. 'I believe that we shall have a most satisfactory marriage,' he told her, and bent to kiss her—a quick, gentle kiss, so that she really didn't have time to enjoy it.

'I'll take you back now. I'm operating in the morning tomorrow; could you get up in time for tea? We can have it together; we have a great deal to talk about. When do you get nights off?'

'In four nights' time.'

'I may be in Bristol, but I'll come and see you at your home if your mother does not mind.' He thought for a moment. 'I shall be able to drive you home before I go.'

'There's no need,' began Sophie, and stopped when he said quietly,

'But I should like to, Sophie.'

He saw her to her door, remarking that he was un-likely to see her until her nights off, and drove away, leaving her to parry Miss Phipps's avid questions before she escaped upstairs to her room and Mabel's unde-manding company.

Curled up in bed presently, nicely drowsy after her splendid breakfast, she admitted that she had been glad to see Rijk again. She thought it very likely that they might not see eye to eye about a number of things, but they weren't things which mattered. She looked forward to a well ordered and contented future, free from the anguish of falling in love and being rejected. She and Rijk were sensible, level-headed people prepared to make a success of a marriage based on friendship and a high regard for each other.

Upon which lofty and erroneous thoughts she went happily to sleep.

Two mornings later, when she was on her way to breakfast, she was asked to go to the office. She might leave, Matron told her graciously. Professor van Taak ter Wijsma had asked that the usual formalities of leaving might be overlooked, since he had to return to Holland shortly and was desirous of taking Sophie with him. Matron's features relaxed into a rare smile. 'I hope you will be very happy, Sister. The professor is a splendid man and very well liked here. He comes here frequently, as you know, so I hope that we shall see something of you from time to time.'

Sophie murmured suitably and got herself out of the room and started on the rambling passages which would take her to the canteen and breakfast. She didn't hurry; she had too much to think about, strolling along,

contemplating her shoes while she viewed the future.
Which meant that she didn't see Rijk until he stopped
in front of her.

'Good morning, Sophie.' He appeared to be in no
hurry. 'Have you been to the office yet?'

She nodded. 'Yes, just this minute. Matron was very
nice; she said that I might leave whenever it was convenient for you...'

'And you,' he pointed out gravely. 'I shall be going
back in five days' time; will you come with me and see
what you think of Holland and my home? And if you
feel you want to change your mind, no hard feelings,
Sophie.'

He smiled then. 'You're on your way to breakfast,
aren't you? And I'm expected in Theatre. I'll be outside
on the day you leave. *Tot ziens.*'

She watched his vast back disappear down the corridor and hoped that *tot ziens* meant something nice like
'lovely to see you'. He had been rather businesslike, but
probably he had his mind on his work...

She sat down at the breakfast-table, her mind full of
all the things she had to do before she left, and the first
one was to tell everyone at the table...

'I'm leaving in four days' time,' she announced during
a pause in the talk, and, when they all looked at her in
astonishment, hurried on, 'I didn't know until just now—
it's been arranged specially. I'm going to marry Professor
van Taak ter Wijsma and I'm going over to Holland to
meet his family.'

The chorus of ohs and aahs was very gratifying; she
was well liked, and only Gill looked disappointed,
although she brightened presently. 'When you're married

you can invite me to stay; there must be lots of people like him out there.'

Everyone laughed and then fell to congratulating Sophie and asking questions. She had to say that she didn't know to most of them. She wasn't even sure where Rijk was, only that he would be waiting for her when he had said.

There was so much to arrange; Mabel would have to be taken home while she was away, and she supposed that she would go home herself when they came back from visiting Rijk's home in Holland, and that would mean telling Miss Phipps. Unable to face that lady's curiosity, she stopped at a phone box on the way back to her flatlet and rang her mother.

Her parent's voice sounded pleased. 'I—your father too—think that you will be very happy; is there anything that you want me to do? It's rather short notice.'

'My passport—and would you just be a dear and look after Mabel? I've no idea where Rijk is, only that he said he'd see me on the day I leave. I'm leaving in four days' time. It's all a bit sudden, but he seems to have arranged things.'

'You're happy, love?'

'Yes, Mother. I'm a bit scared of meeting his family— all those sisters... Supposing they don't like me?'

'You're marrying Rijk, love, not his sisters. I'm sure it will be all right.'

Her mother's voice was reassuring.

She had very little time to make plans; the junior night sister was to take over from her and Staff Nurse Pitt was to be made junior night sister in her place. The three of them had been working together for a year or two, so there was little need to explain things to them. Sophie rushed through an inventory with one of the office sisters, staying behind after breakfast and going back to her room long after she should have been in bed, to find an indignant Mabel waiting for her and an inquisitive Miss Phipps, still unaware of her impending departure. Sophie, falling into bed, stayed awake long enough to decide that since Rijk was arranging everything with such speed he could deal with her landlady too.

He was waiting for her after her last night on duty. She had been and paid a last visit to Matron's office, said goodbye to her friends and also to Peter Small and Tim and the porters, and now, burdened by various farewell gifts, she went through the hospital doors for the last time.

The professor got out of his car and came to meet her. He took her packages and put them in the car and asked, 'What do you want to do first? We will be going over on the night ferry tomorrow; would it be a good idea if we go to your room and, while you collect Mabel and whatever you need, I'll see to Miss Phipps? I'll keep your room for a week or so so that when we get back you can come and pack up the rest of your things. That will give you the rest of today to sleep and put a few things in a case. I'll come for you tomorrow about six o'clock; we're going from Harwich...'

'You've thought of everything... How long will we be in Holland?'

'A week—I have to go to Leeds for a couple of days and then Athens. I'll bring you back here first; you'll want to be home for Christmas. I'm not sure how long I shall be there, but I'll come as soon as I can...'

'You'll be there for Christmas?'

'I rather think so.' He popped her into the car. 'But let us get you settled first before we discuss that.'

He was as good as his word and so Sophie, coming downstairs half an hour later with a hastily packed case and Mabel in her basket, found Miss Phipps waiting in the hall. The professor took her case from her and went out to the car and Miss Phipps said excitedly, 'Oh, my goodness, Sister, dear, what a romantic surprise— whoever would have thought it? Though I must say I did wonder... And don't worry about your flatlet; I'll keep it locked until you come back to get the rest of your things.' Her wig slipped a little to one side in her excitement. 'I don't know when I've had such a thrill.'

Sophie murmured suitably, assured her landlady that she would be back within a week or so, and bade her goodbye.

'You'll make a lovely bride,' breathed Miss Phipps as Sophie went out to the car.

The professor was leaning against the gate, looking relaxed. He was a man, Sophie reflected, who seemed to make himself comfortable wherever he was. He looked as though he hadn't an anxiety in the world. The thought reminded her that she hadn't either. She got into the car and he shut the door and got in beside her, glancing at his watch. 'Your mother said she would have coffee ready at eleven o'clock.' He turned to smile at her then and she thought how pleasant it was to feel so at ease with someone. At the same time it struck her that she was being swept along by his well laid plans even though never once had they caused her inconvenience or given her reason to grumble.

'Have you been up all night again?' she asked him sharply.

He slowed the Bentley at the traffic lights and glanced at her, smiling a little. 'You sound very wifely. I slept on the ferry.'

'I didn't mean to nag...'

'If that is nagging I rather liked it.'

Her mother was waiting for them, with coffee on the table and a large newly baked cake, and ten minutes later with Mabel sitting between the dogs, Mercury and Montgomery, before the Aga, they were sitting around the kitchen table.

'You'll stay for lunch?' asked Mrs Blount.

'I've one or two things to see to, Mrs Blount. I'll be here tomorrow evening to fetch Sophie—we're going over on the Harwich ferry and that will give me all day...'

'You couldn't spend Christmas with us?'

'I would have liked that. I shall be in Greece, although I shall do my best to get back to my home even if only for a day.'

'You poor man,' said Mrs Blount, and meant it.

He went presently, saying all the right things to her and giving Sophie a quick, almost brotherly kiss as he went.

'You are happy about marrying Rijk?' asked her mother as they went back indoors.

'We're not in love or anything like that, Mother. It's just that we... He wants a wife and we get on very well together and I do like him very much.' Sophie gave her mother a worried look. 'Rijk says that a good marriage depends on friendship and liking and that just falling in love isn't enough.' She filled their coffee-mugs again and sat down at the table. 'I've been afraid of falling in love ever since...'

'Yes, dear, I understand. As long as you aren't still in love—it is a long time ago.'

'I told Rijk I can't remember his face or anything about him, but I remember how I felt. I've been so careful to avoid getting too friendly with any of the men I've met. Somehow Rijk is different... I'm not explaining very well, am I?'

'No need, Sophie, dear. It seems to me that you are ideally suited to each other. Rijk is old and wise enough to know what he wants and so are you. I am quite sure that you will be happy together.'

Mrs Blount gave her daughter a loving look. The dear girl had no idea; it was a good thing that the professor was a man of patience and determination and that he had the ability to hide his feelings so successfully. Once they were married he would doubtless set about the task of making Sophie fall in love with him. She nodded her head and smiled, and Sophie, looking up, asked what was amusing her.

'I was thinking about a really splendid hat for your wedding, dear,' said her mother guilelessly. 'And, talking of hats, if you are not too tired, shall we go upstairs and look through your wardrobe? Pick out what you want to take with you and I'll get it pressed.'

A good deal of the rest of the day was taken up with the knotty problem of what to wear. Her Jaeger suit, Sophie decided; she could travel in it and it would look right during the day with a handful of blouses. A short dress for the evening—a rich mulberry silk, very plain with long sleeves and a straight skirt. And upon due reflection she added a midnight-blue velvet dress with a long skirt, very full, tiny sleeves and a low neckline.

'Take that jersey dress as well,' suggested her mother, so she added still another garment, dark green this time with a cowl neckline and a pleated skirt.

'It's bound to rain or snow or something,' said Sophie, and folded a quilted jacket with a hood, adding sensible shoes, thick gloves and a woolly cap, with the vague idea that Friesland sounded as though it might be cold in winter.

'I'll pack tomorrow,' she told her mother. 'Will Father be home for lunch?'

'Yes, dear, and this afternoon shouldn't you have a nap?'

She wasn't at all sleepy, Sophie decided, obediently curling up on her bed that afternoon; there was so much to think about. The next thing she knew was her mother's hand on her shoulder.

'A cup of tea, love, and supper will be about half an hour.'

She went to bed rather early, her hair washed, her face anointed with a cream guaranteed to erase all lines and wrinkles, determined to look her best for Rijk's family. It was to be hoped, she thought sleepily, that not all the five sisters would be there. And his brothers—would they be there too?

She fell asleep uneasily, suddenly beset by doubts.

There was no time for doubts the next day; there was the packing to do, the dogs to take for a walk, a last-minute anxious inspection of her handbag, and her father to drive to a nearby farm to attend a cow calving with difficulty. They got back home in time for tea and then it was time for her to go upstairs and dress for the journey. Rijk had said that he would come in the early evening, and she knew that the ferry sailed before midnight. The drive to Harwich wouldn't take much more than an hour, and her mother had supper ready.

He arrived while she was still in her room, studying her lovely face in the looking-glass, anxious that she should look her best, and, hearing the car and the murmur of voices in the hall, she hurried downstairs to find him, his overcoat off, sitting with her father. He got up as she went into the room and came to take her hand and give her a light kiss.

'I see that you are ready,' he observed. 'Your mother has kindly invited me to share your supper—we don't need to leave for an hour or so.'

'I'll go and help her,' said Sophie, suddenly anxious to be gone when only a few moments earlier she had been equally anxious to see him again. It was silly to feel shy with him; she supposed it was because she was excited about going to Holland. She joined her mother in the kitchen and carried plates of hot sausage rolls, jacket potatoes, mince pies and toasted sandwiches into the dining-room. There was coffee too and beer for the men, although the professor shook his head regretfully over that, at the same time embarking on a discussion with Mr Blount concerning the merits of various beers. Sophie, while glad that her father and Rijk got on so well together, couldn't help feeling a faint resentment at the professor's matter-of-fact manner towards her. After all, they were going to be married, weren't they? Surely he could show a little more interest in his future wife? Upon reflection, she had to admit that their marriage wasn't quite the romantic affair everyone, even Matron, had envisaged, and Rijk wasn't a man to pretend...

They left after a leisurely meal and the promise on Sophie's part that she would let her mother know that they had arrived safely.

'You can phone,' said the professor, 'during the morning.' He smiled at Mrs Blount. 'I'll take good care of her, Mrs Blount.'

Her mother leaned through the car window and kissed his cheek. 'I know that. Have a good trip and a happy week together.'

The ferry was half empty; they had more coffee and then parted for the night. 'I've told the stewardess to bring you tea and toast at six o'clock,' said Rijk. 'Sleep well, Sophie.'

It was rough on the crossing and, although she didn't feel seasick, she lay and worried, wishing that she had never agreed to meet his family, never agreed to marry him, for that matter, never allowed him to foster their friendship in the first place...

She drank her tea and ate the toast and dressed, somewhat restored in her spirits in the light of a grey overcast morning. She was looking out of the porthole when there was a knock on the door and the professor came in. He took a look at her face and flung an arm round her shoulders. 'You've been awake all night wishing you had never met me, never said that probably you will marry me, never agreed to come home with me.'

He gave her a sudden kiss, not at all like the swift kisses he had given her, but hard and warm, and her spirits rose with it. 'Haven't you any doubts at all?' she asked him.

'Not one. We're about to dock. Come along, you'll feel better once we're on dry land.'

Strangely enough she did, relieved that her vague disquiet had melted away; she felt comfortable with him again, asking questions about the country that they were passing through.

'We'll stop for coffee,' he told her. 'It's about a hundred and forty miles to my home; we should be there soon after eleven o'clock. We shall be on the motorway for most of the time—not very interesting, I'm afraid, but quick.'

The road ahead was straight with no hills in sight, bypassing the towns and villages. Holland was exactly as she had pictured it: flat and green with a wide sky and far more built-up than she had expected.

'This is the busiest corner of the country,' Rijk explained. 'The further north we go, the fewer towns and factories. I think that you will like Friesland.'

They stopped for their coffee before they crossed the Afsluitdijk and by now, although it wasn't raining, there was a strong wind blowing, so that the water looked grey and cold.

The country had changed. They were across the *dijk* now and Rijk had taken a right-hand fork on to a motorway, passing Bolsward and circumventing Sneek before turning on to a country road. Villages were few and far between in the rolling countryside, but there were a few farmhouses, backed by huge barns, standing well apart from each other. In the distance a glimpse of water was visible.

'The sea?' asked Sophie, vague as to their direction.

'The lakes; Friesland is riddled with them. In the summer they're crowded with boats. That's Sneeker Meer you can see now. Presently we will go through a small town called Grouw, past more lakes. I live in a village well away from everywhere. We're going there first. Later we will go to my parents' home in Leeuwarden; that's only twelve miles or so.'

She was thankful to hear that. 'Will they be there? All your family?'

He gave her clasped hands on her lap a brief comforting squeeze.

'They will like you and you will like them.'

'Oh, I do so hope so. Is this Grouw?'

It was really a very large village on the edge of a small lake and with a small harbour. In the summer it would be delightful, she thought; even now on this grey day it was picturesque and the small houses looked cosy. There were a few shops too and a hotel by the harbour. She craned her neck to see as much as possible before the professor drove into a narrow road with another lake on one side and a canal on the other, to cross a narrow spit of land and turn north and presently back towards the shore of a much larger lake.

'This is the Prinsenhof lake—the village is called Eernewoude; I live just the other side of it. Very quiet in winter, but watersports in summer.'

'There aren't any hospitals near—doesn't it take you a long time to reach them?'

'We're still only twelve miles from Leeuwarden, where I have beds, and Groningen is less than thirty miles—I have beds there too. I can reach the motorway to the south easily—Amsterdam is only a hundred miles and the Belgian-Dutch border another sixty miles or so.'

'Do you go abroad a lot? Other than England?'

'Fairly frequently.' They were driving slowly through the village—a handful of houses, a church, a small shop, and then a narrow brick road, the water on one side, a brick wall on the other, with great wrought-iron gates halfway along its length. They were open and a drive curved away, bordered by dense bushes and bare trees. The house was at the end of the curve and when Sophie saw it she took a sharp breath at the sight of it. She hadn't known what to expect, certainly not this imposing house of red brick and sandstone with its steep tiled roof, tall chimneys and square central tower surmounted by more tiles and an onion dome. It sheltered the vast door. The windows were long and narrow with painted shutters and to one side of the house there was what she took to be a moat.

The professor had stopped before his door and got out, opened her door and taken her arm.

He said in a comforting kind of voice, 'It's quite cosy inside.'

Sophie looked up at him. 'It's beautiful—I had no idea. I am longing to go in; I can't wait—and there's a dog barking...'

He smiled down at her excited face. 'Come inside and meet Matt.'

CHAPTER FIVE

SOPHIE and Rijk climbed the shallow steps to the door together and it was opened as they reached it to allow a large shaggy dog to launch itself at the professor. Sophie prudently took a step back, for the animal was large and looked ferocious as well. The professor bore the onslaught with equanimity, bade the beast calm down, and drew Sophie forward.

'This is Matt. A bouvier. He'll be your companion, your devoted friend, and die for you if he has to.'

Sophie took off her glove and offered a balled fist and the beast sniffed at it and then rasped it with a great tongue. He had small yellow eyes and enormous teeth, but she had the impression that he was smiling at her. Indeed, he offered his head for a friendly scratch.

The man who had opened the door was as unlike Percy as it was possible to be, a powerfully built man with a slight stoop, grey hair and a round, weather-beaten face. The professor shook hands with him and clapped him on the shoulder and introduced him.

'This is Rauke, who looks after the house. His wife, Tyske, housekeeps and cooks; here she comes.'

Sophie shook hands with Rauke and then with the elderly woman who had joined them in the porch. She was as tall as Sophie, with a long face and grey hair and clear blue eyes. Her handshake was firm and she said something with a smile which Sophie hoped was a welcome.

The porch opened into a vestibule which in turn opened into the hall, square and white-walled, with a staircase facing the door, lighted by a long window on its half-landing. The ceiling was lofty and from it hung a brass chandelier, simple in design and, thought Sophie, very old. There was an elaborately carved side-table too and two great chairs arranged on either side of it. It was exactly like a Dutch interior, even to the black and white marble floor. Still gazing around her, she was led away by Tyske to a cloakroom under the staircase, equipped with every modern comfort. She had time to think while she did her face and tidied her hair, and back in the hall she said at once, 'You might have told me, Rijk.'

'What should I have told you?' He looked amused.

'Why, that you had such a grand house. I don't know what I expected, but it wasn't this.'

'It is my home,' he said simply, 'and it isn't grand— on the large side, perhaps, but I use all the rooms—not all the time, of course, but I live here, Sophie. Come and have a cup of coffee and presently we will go over it together.'

He ushered her through a double door into a room with windows overlooking the grounds at the back of the house. It was light by reason of the lofty ceiling and was furnished with sofas and easy-chairs arranged around the hooded fireplace, in which a fire burned briskly. The walls were panelled and hung with faded red silk and there were a great many paintings on them, mostly portraits. There were glass-fronted cabinets against the walls, filled with porcelain and silver, and a handsome Stoel clock hanging above the fireplace, and scattered around, with a nice regard for the convenience of the room's occupants, were small tables with elegant table lamps.

Matt came to meet them as they crossed to the fire and once they were seated facing each other he stretched out between them, breathing gusty sighs of content, one eye on the coffee-tray and the plate of biscuits beside it.

They drank their coffee in companionable silence broken only by the crunching of the biscuits the professor offered to Matt.

'He must miss you,' said Sophie.

'Oh, yes. He goes with me to Leeuwarden and Groningen, though. He will be delighted to have your company while I'm away.'

'You don't have to go away?'

The dismay on her face made him say at once, 'No, no. I was talking of when we are married.' He put down his coffee-cup and sat back at his ease. 'We have a whole week to be together, Sophie.'

And at the uncertain look on her face, 'My mother and father will come back here and stay with us for a week. They have many friends living around here; they will be out every day.' He grinned suddenly. 'You see how careful I am to observe the proprieties—unnecessary in this day and age, but we're a strait-laced lot in Friesland.'

Sophie, with a slightly heightened colour, looked him in the eye. 'I'm strait-laced too.'

'Which strengthens my argument that we are very well suited.'

He got up and Matt got up with him. 'Would you like to see the house?'

They crossed the hall with Matt keeping pace with them, and the professor opened a door on its opposite side. 'The dining-room,' he told her, 'but when I'm on my own I use a smaller room at the back of the house. I have asked Rauke to set lunch there for us.'

It was a splendid room; she could imagine a dinner party sitting around the rectangular table, decked no doubt with silver and crystal, and with the wall sconces sending a flattering glow on the women guests. There was a sideboard along one wall with flanking pedestal cupboards surmounted by urns and several large oil-paintings hung on the walls; a second door led to a smaller room—a kind of ante-room, she supposed. In turn it opened into a room at the back of the house with doors opening on to the terrace from which steps led to wide lawns and flowerbeds. It was a charming room, furnished with easy-chairs and a circular table; there was a television set in one corner and bookshelves and a dear little writing-table in another corner. There was a bright fire burning here and the professor declared, 'This is one of my favourite rooms—we shall lunch here, just the two of us.'

He opened a door beside the windows. 'This is the library.' It was a splendid room with enormous desks at each end of it, leather chairs arranged around small tables, and shelves of books.

'One more room,' he observed and led her through a door into the hall again and opened a door close to the staircase. 'My study.'

It was austerely furnished with a partners' desk, a vast leather chair behind it, a couple of smaller chairs facing it and again shelves of books. There was a computer, too, an electric typewriter and an answering machine all arranged on a smaller table under the two long windows.

'I have a secretary who comes three or four times a week and sees to my letters.' He flipped over the pile of correspondence on his desk. 'Let us go upstairs.'

The staircase was of oak with a wrought-iron balustrade with a half-landing from where it branched to the gallery above. It was quiet there, their footsteps deadened by the thick carpet as he led her to the front of the house. There were a pair of rather grand double doors here and he opened them on to a beautiful room, the vast bed and furniture of satin wood, the curtains and bedspread of ivory and rose brocade. Sophie rotated slowly, looking her fill.

'What a beautiful room. You have a lovely home, Rijk—it's a bit big, but it's so—lived-in.'

'I'm glad you like it. Come this way.' He opened a door to a bathroom which led in turn to a smaller bedroom and then into the corridor.

There were passages leading to the back of the house and he led her down each one in turn, opening doors so that she might look at each room before going up a smaller flight of stairs to the floor above.

The rooms were smaller here but just as comfortably furnished, and right at the end of one passage there was a large, airy room with bars at the windows and a high fireguard before the big stove. There was a rocking-horse under the windows and a doll's house on one of the numerous shelves. Sophie wondered what toys the closed cupboards held.

'Your nanny must have had a busy time,' she observed. 'You and your brothers and sisters...'

'She stood no nonsense and we all loved her dearly. You shall meet her later on—she has her own rooms in my parents' house. The night nurseries are through there as well as a room for Nanny and a little kitchen. We spent a great deal of time with my mother and father— we all had a very happy childhood.'

They were back in the passage with Matt, breathing heavily with pleasure, at their heels when a gong sounded from below. 'Lunch,' said the professor. 'There's still another floor, but we can look at that later on.'

They talked about nothing much as they ate; the professor steadfastly refused to allow Sophie to ask questions of a personal nature and since she was hungry and the leek soup, bacon fritters and assortment of vegetables were very much to her taste she didn't much mind.

It was like being in a dream, she reflected, pouring coffee for them both; any minute she would wake up and find herself back in the accident room at St Agnes's...

They got into the car presently with Matt crouching in the back, poking his great head between them from time to time and giving great gusty sighs.

'Does he like cats?' asked Sophie.

'I have been told over and over again by well meaning people that he would kill any cat he saw. He takes no notice of them at all; indeed, he is on the best of terms with Tyske's Miep and her kittens, and Miep doesn't care tuppence for him.'

They were on the motorway now, racing towards Leeuwarden, and Sophie stared out of the window, a bundle of nerves.

Without looking at her, the professor began a rambling conversation about Matt which needed no replies and which lasted until he slowed the car to drive through the heart of Leeuwarden. The afternoon was darkening already and the shops were lighted, decked for Christmas, and the pavements were thronged with shoppers, but she didn't have much chance to look around her for Rijk turned away from the main streets and drove through narrow ways lined with tall old houses and then into a brick street beside a canal with a line of great gabled houses facing it. He stopped before one of them.

'Here we are,' he told her.

The man who opened the door to them was elderly, tall and thin, but very upright. He greeted the professor with a dignified, 'A pleasure to see you, Mr Rijk, sir,' and Rijk shook his hand and clapped him on the shoulder.

'How are you, Clerkie? Sophie, this is Clerk, who runs this place for my father and mother—has done for as long as I can remember—taught me to fish and swim and ride a bike—taught us all, in fact.'

Sophie put out a hand and he went on, 'Miss Sophie Blount, my guest for a week. Anyone at home?'

Clerk's calm features broke into a smile. 'Everyone, sir.' He gave Sophie a fatherly look. 'Shall I take Miss Blount's coat? And would she wish to arrange her hair and so forth?'

The professor turned to study her. 'Not a hair out of place and the face looks much as usual. You'll do, Sophie.' He took her arm and crossed the square hall with Clerk's figure slightly ahead to open the door on one side of it.

The room was large, with a high ceiling and enormous windows stretching from ceiling to floor; it was also full of people, children and dogs.

As they went in the loud murmurs of conversation stopped and there was a surge towards them with cries of 'Rijk' and a babble of talk Sophie couldn't understand, but the next minute she found herself face to face with the professor's parents, his arm tucked comfortably under hers.

At first glance Mevrouw van Taak ter Wijsma looked formidable, but that was by reason of her height and well corseted stoutness. A second glance was more reassuring; her blue eyes, on a level with Sophie's, were kind and the smile on her still handsome face was sweet. She was dressed elegantly, her grey hair swept into an old-fashioned coil on top of her head, her twin set and skirt very much in the same style as that of Sophie's mother. It was silly that such a small thing should have put Sophie at her ease.

The professor's father was still a very handsome man with white hair and dark eyes. He kissed Sophie's cheek and welcomed her with a warmth she hadn't expected, before Rijk led her around the room. His five sisters were there, and so were their husbands, their children and a variety of dogs; moreover, his two brothers were there too. She shook hands and smiled and forgot all their names the moment they were said, but that didn't seem to matter in such an atmosphere of friendliness. As for the children, they clung to their uncle, offered small hands and cheeks for a kiss and took her for granted. So did the dogs—two Labradors, a Jack Russell and a small whiskery creature with melting eyes. His name was Friday, she was told, and when she asked why one of the older children said in English, 'That was the day Daddy found him.' They asked, 'We have cats; do you?'

'Well, yes, I have a cat of my own; she's called Mabel.'

'Good, you will bring her here when you marry Uncle Rijk?'

'Well, yes. You speak very good English...'

'We have a nanny. When you and Oom Rijk have babies you will also have a nanny.'

The conversation was getting rather out of hand; she looked round for Rijk and caught his eye and he broke off the conversation with his father and made his way to her. 'Is Timon practising his English? He's Tiele's eldest son—she's the one in the green dress. Three boys so far, but they'd like a daughter... Come and talk to Loewert. He's at Leiden in his last year.'

He was a younger edition of Rijk and brimming over with the wish to be friendly. He obligingly took her round the room once more and told her all the names once again so that by the time they had all settled round the room drinking tea and eating fragile little biscuits she could pick out various members of the family for herself. Rijk's mother, sitting beside her on one of the massive sofas, was carrying on the kind of conversation which didn't need much thought, telling her little snippets of information about the family.

'We are such a large family,' she observed, 'and I am sure that Rijk quite forgot to tell you about us. He is immersed in his work—too much so, I consider.' She smiled at Sophie. 'You will alter that, I hope, my dear.'

Sophie, watching him talking to his brothers at the other end of the room, wondered if she would. It seemed unlikely.

Presently they got up to go. Rijk's parents went away to get their hats and coats, Matt was coaxed away from the garden where he had been romping with the other dogs, and Sophie began a round of goodbyes. She hadn't known about the Dutch kissing three times; by the time she had bidden goodbye to everyone in the room she felt quite giddy. She must remember to ask Rijk about it; he had never kissed her three times. Indeed, his kisses had been few and far between and then brief...

The elders of the party got into the back of the Bentley with Matt and Sophie found herself sitting by Rijk, and really, she thought a little crossly, I've hardly seen him all afternoon.

He seemed unaware of her coolness, though, talking about his family in a desultory way until they reached his house and once they were there seeing to his parents' comfort, handing them over to Rauke, and then walking her off to the small sitting-room at the back of the house.

'There's half an hour before we need to change,' he told her. 'Come and have a drink and tell me what you think of my family.'

'They are very nice,' said Sophie inadequately. 'I haven't quite sorted them out yet...'

'Time enough to do that,' he said cheerfully. 'Would you like a glass of sherry? We'll meet in the drawing-room just before dinner, but I think you deserve a drink; the family like you.'

'Supposing they hadn't liked me?'

He shrugged huge shoulders. 'That would make no difference as far as I'm concerned.'

He turned away to pour the sherry and she said on impulse, 'Have you ever been in love, Rijk?'

He put the drink down beside her and settled into a chair opposite hers.

'Several times! If you mean the fleeting romances we are all prone to from time to time. But if you are doubtful as to any future entanglements of that nature on my part, I can assure you that I have long outgrown them.'

Once started she persisted. 'But you do believe in people falling in love and—and loving each other?'

'Certainly I do. For those fortunate enough to do both.' He added softly, 'Cold feet, Sophie?'

'No, no.' She blushed a little under his amused gaze. 'I was just being curious; I didn't mean to pry.'

'I'm glad we're good friends enough to be able to ask each other such questions.'

'Yes, well, so am I. I think I'd better go up and change...'

'I must take a quick turn in the garden with Matt. We'll meet again in the drawing-room.'

He got up with her and opened the door and stood watching her as she crossed the hall and started up the staircase. Sophie, aware of that, felt self-conscious, which wasn't like her at all.

She wore the mulberry silk; it suited her well and, studying her reflection in the pier glass, she felt tolerably satisfied with her appearance. She hadn't been quite sure what to wear, but somehow Rijk's mother looked the kind of lady to follow the conventions of her younger days. She was glad that she had decided to wear it when she entered the drawing-room, for Mevrouw van Taak ter Wijsma was in black crêpe, cut with great elegance, and a fitting background for the double row of pearls she was wearing. As for the men, they wore dark grey suits and ties of subdued splendour, so that Sophie felt that she was dressed exactly as she ought to be and heaved a small sigh of relief, noticed with the ghost of a smile by Rijk.

The evening was pleasant; the dinner was superb: mushrooms in garlic, roast duck with an orange sauce, lemon syllabub and a *bombe glacée* to finish.

Getting up from the table, Sophie wondered if the meal was a sample of the week ahead. If so, she would have to take long walks or do exercises in her room each morning.

She didn't have to worry about the exercises; the next morning Rijk took her walking and she was glad of the sensible shoes and a thick woolly under the Jaeger jacket, for the weather was cold and the sky grey with a wind which hinted at snow later on. He took her briskly round the grounds and then down to the village beyond, with Matt prancing along beside them. As they walked he talked about his home and the life he led.

'I am away a good deal,' he told her, 'you know that already, but I come home whenever I can. Of course, if you wish you can accompany me to England when I go and visit your parents while I am working. You won't be lonely if you stay here; the family will see to that, and besides, you will soon make friends.'

It seemed to her that he was making it clear that he didn't want her with him while he travelled away from home. Reasonable enough, she supposed, it wasn't as though he was head over heels in love with her; theirs was to be a placid, well mannered marriage with no strong feelings, and she supposed that was what she wanted. She had told him that, hadn't she? He had taken her at her word, no doubt content to have found a woman who had the same attitude to marriage as he had.

They walked until lunchtime and had that meal together, for his mother and father had gone to visit neighbouring friends and wouldn't be back until the evening. When they had finished Rijk asked her if she would like to go with him to his study while he looked over the notes on several cases he had been asked to deal with. She was surprised, but settled down in a comfortable leather chair by the window with a pile of magazines, while Matt got under the desk at his master's feet.

The room was pleasantly warm and very quiet and she took care not to speak, even when she glanced out of the window and saw the first snowflakes falling, and presently she had her reward, for the professor closed his case papers and leaned back in his chair. 'How restful you are, Sophie; I'm sure you were longing to tell me that it was snowing...'

'Well, yes, I was, but I know how annoying it is when you're studying something or writing a report and someone keeps talking in hushed tones or sighing.'

'I can see we're ideally suited. Come and have tea; you deserve a whole pot to yourself.'

His parents came back presently and they dined and spent the rest of the evening sitting in the drawing-room. Mevrouw van Taak ter Wijsma made no bones about questioning Sophie, in the nicest possible way, about her life and home. Sophie answered readily enough; if she were a mother, even if her son were an adult well able to look after his own interests, she felt sure that she would want to know as much as possible about a future daughter-in-law.

Rijk followed her out into the hall when she and his mother went to bed. 'Shall we walk again in the morning?' he asked her. 'I'm going to Leeuwarden after lunch; perhaps you would like to come with me? You can look around the shops while I am at the hospital.'

She agreed readily, and presently, in bed and half asleep, began on a list of presents she would take home with her. She was asleep before it was even half finished.

They walked away from the village in the morning, taking a narrow cart track which wound round the shores of the lake, and Sophie, muffled in her coat and with her head swathed in a cashmere scarf of Rijk's, was glad of them, for the wind was cutting and the snow, long ceased, had frozen on the ground. Looking around her, she had to admit that the scenery was bleak, and yet she liked it. Which, she conceded silently, was a good thing if she were to marry Rijk. She hadn't made up her mind yet, she reminded herself, despite his cool assumption that their marriage was a foregone conclusion.

Even while she thought about it, she knew in her heart of hearts that she would marry him; he would be a good husband, kind and considerate and undemanding, and more than anything else she wanted the security and contentment which he had offered her. Romance, she had decided wistfully, wasn't for her. Her only taste of it had turned sour; far better settle for a comfortable relationship.

He drove her to Leeuwarden in the afternoon, set her down in the centre of the shopping centre, close to the ancient Weigh House, told her that he would wait there for her at four o'clock, and drove himself off to the hospital.

Left to herself, Sophie studied the shop windows and presently made a few purchases. Cigars for her father, a Delft blue vase for her mother, a thick slab of chocolate for Tom and, after a lengthy search, a book on Friesland for George, who was a bookworm, and a pen and pencil set for Paul. She could have bought that in England, but at least it was in a Dutch box and the description was in that language, which made it rather different.

By then it was getting on for four o'clock and she made her way back to the Weigh House and found Rijk waiting. He took her parcels from her, settled her in the car and got in beside her. 'You found shopping easy enough?' he wanted to know.

'Well, yes; once or twice I got a bit muddled, but almost everyone speaks English. Did you have a busy afternoon?'

'An unusual case...' He began to tell her about it and she listened with intelligence and real interest, so that he observed, 'How delightful it is to discuss my work with someone who knows what I'm talking about and is really interested.'

Which gave Sophie a gentle glow of pleasure.

The next day he put her in the car and took her on a sightseeing tour of Friesland. North first, to Dokkum, where they had coffee at a nice old-fashioned hotel by the canal, and then on to the coast and the Waddenzee, bleak and cold, with a distant view of the islands, looking lonely beyond the dull grey sea.

'Do people live there?' asked Sophie.

'Good heavens, yes. In summer they swarm with holiday-makers. They're very peaceful out of season; there are bird sanctuaries and beautiful beaches. We will go in early spring and you shall see for yourself.'

He drove south again along narrow brick roads built on their dikes, bypassed Leeuwarden, and stopped in Franeker, where they had a lunch of *erwtensoep*, a thick pea soup, rich with pieces of sausage and pork, followed by smoked eel on toast—the kind of food, Rijk assured Sophie, which kept the sometimes very cold winter at bay.

They sat over their coffee until a watery sun decided him that it would be worth going down the coast to Hindeloopen and Staveren before turning for home.

Even on a winter's day, Hindeloopen was charming. They walked along the sea wall before driving on to Staveren, which disappointed her so much that Rijk drove inland to Sloten; the sixteenth-century charm of the tiny town more than made up for the unattractiveness of Staveren.

It was dusk as they arrived back at the house, and the windows glowed with light. The professor got out and opened Sophie's door as Rauke, already on the porch, stood back to allow Matt to hurl himself at his master, and she stood quietly, looking around her.

In the fast-gathering dark the house looked beautiful and a little awe-inspiring. There was already a touch of frost on the lawn before it and the trees surrounding it were rustling and sighing. She wondered how long they had been standing there, guarding the house. After her happy and contented day she felt suddenly uncertain; if it hadn't been for Rauke standing there in the cold waiting for them to go inside she would have unburdened herself to Rijk there and then; as it was she went into the house and allowed Rijk to take her coat before she went to her room to tidy her hair and do things to her face. It glowed with the cold air and her eyes sparkled, but it didn't mirror her feelings. She went down to the sitting-room, where the professor was waiting for her, the tea-tray with its shining silver and delicate china already on the sofa table.

Much though she wanted a cup of tea, she had made up her mind to say what she had to say first. She began at once. 'Rijk...'

He looked up from the letters he was glancing through and studied her face. 'Something is worrying you, Sophie?'

'Yes, how did you know?'

He said quietly, 'We are friends—close friends—are we not, my dear?'

'Yes, oh, yes, we are. I'm a bit worried. You see, I didn't know about all this.' She waved a hand around her at the understated comfort and luxury around them. 'I knew you were a very successful man; I supposed that you would have a nice house in Holland and be—well, comfortably off. But this is different. Are you very rich?'

His firm mouth twitched. 'I'm afraid so. I can only plead that a good deal of my wealth is the result of no doubt ill gotten gains from my merchant ancestors.'

She nodded like a child, glad to have had something explained. 'Yes, I see. You don't think that I am marrying you for your money, Rijk?'

He said gently, 'No, Sophie, I don't think that.'

'Because I'm not. Money's nice to have, isn't it? But it isn't as important as other things. If—if I say I'll marry you it wouldn't make any difference to me if you were on the dole.'

He crossed the room to where she was still standing and took both her hands in his, bent his head, and kissed her. A gentle kiss, as gentle as his voice had been. It reassured her so that she said, 'Well, that's all right, then, isn't it?'

'Perfectly all right. Come and pour the tea and I'll tell you what I have to do tomorrow.'

He was going to Brussels to examine some highly connected man with a suspected brain tumour. 'I shall be away all day. Mother and Father would like you to go with them on a visit to my grandmother—she lives in Heerenveen—for lunch and tea. I hope to be back in time for dinner.'

'You aren't going to drive all that way there and back?' She sounded, did she but know it, like an anxious wife, and he smiled.

'No, I shall fly. I have a light plane I use from time to time.'

'You can fly as well?'

'It saves a great deal of time. Do you drive a car, Sophie?'

'Oh, yes. I take Father round when I'm home; my brothers taught me.'

'Good; we are a little isolated here, but if you have a car you will be able to go where and when you like.' And at her anxious look, he added, 'When I am not at home.'

In bed that night, reviewing her day, she knew that she would marry Rijk. He had, of course, all this time behaved as though she had already agreed to do so, although she was aware that he was prepared to wait for her answer when they got back to England. Her mind made up, there was no point in staying awake; she slept dreamlessly and never heard the plane's engines from a nearby field as Rijk flew off to Brussels.

She was disappointed to find him gone when she went down to breakfast, but, his parents being at the table too, she had no time to brood over that. Bidden to be ready by ten o'clock, she took Matt for a walk in the grounds and joined them in the hall. Rijk's father drove an elderly, beautifully maintained Daimler, and Sophie had expected to be taken at a gentle speed to Heerenveen, but the elderly doctor drove with a speed sometimes alarming on the narrow roads, and since his wife, sitting with Sophie in the back, appeared to find this quite normal, Sophie said nothing, but watched the rolling countryside and made suitable replies to her companions' friendly talk.

Heerenveen was rather nice, she decided as their driver at last slowed down to go through the town and take a narrow road which presently revealed a small lake. Old Mevrouw van Taak ter Wijsma lived in a fair-sized square house close to the water, with a sprinkling of small houses along the road, cared for by several devoted servants. She went out seldom, but kept a sharp eye on her numerous family. She was a tall old lady, very thin, with a high bridged nose and bright blue eyes, dressed in black with a great many gold chains, and she received them in a room overlooking the lake, furnished with old-fashioned heavy furniture, its small tables covered by photos in silver frames, and great cabinets along its walls loaded with beautiful porcelain. She offered a cheek to her son and daughter-in-law and then studied Sophie at some length.

'So you're the girl that Rijk intends to marry. At least you match him with height. Nice-looking too. You'll make him a good wife, no doubt.'

Sophie murmured suitably; there seemed no point in explaining that she hadn't actually said that she would marry Rijk and didn't intend to until he asked her if her mind was made up. She was told to sit by the old lady and spent the next hour making the right replies to that lady's questions.

Lunch was a solemn, long-drawn-out meal and afterwards, their hostess retiring for a brief nap, Sophie was invited to look round the house with Rijk's mother, and by the time they had peered into a great many rather gloomy rooms it was time to join the old lady for milkless tea and very small biscuits.

Presently they drove back to Rijk's home, his father, doubtless pleased at having been able to leave before it was quite dark, driving with a carefree speed which set Sophie's neat head of hair on end.

Rijk was home and came to help his mother and Sophie out of the car while Matt got in everyone's way. As they went indoors he took Sophie's arm.

'And did you like Granny?' he asked. She nodded. 'She's a darling...'

He paused in the hall so that for a moment they were alone. 'She phoned just now; she says you're a darling too.'

For a moment Sophie thought that he would kiss her, but he didn't; he only smiled.

CHAPTER SIX

THERE were only two days left. Sophie went down to breakfast in the morning wondering if Rijk had any plans.

He had: a walk down to the village to meet the dominie and look round the church and then, since it was a clear, cold day, a walk along the lakeside to an outlying farm which he owned. 'And in the afternoon, if you would like, we will drive to Groningen and take a look round—there's a rather splendid church and the university.'

On the way to the village presently he told her that they would go back to his parents' house on the following day, lunch there, and then come back and have an early dinner before driving down to the Hoek to catch the night ferry.

Sophie agreed cheerfully, thankful that she had bought her presents when they had gone to Leeuwarden. 'Do phone your people if you would like to,' went on Rijk. 'We should be back around nine o'clock.'

'Would you like to stay? There's plenty of room—Mother will expect you for lunch, I'm sure.'

'Lunch, by all means, but I've a consultation in the afternoon and I'm operating on the following day and then going to Leeds for a couple of days...'

'But it's almost Christmas...'

'Which I shall have to spend away from home—I did tell you.'

'I forgot. So we can't see each other for a while?'

'No.' He tucked a hand under her elbow. 'May I come and see you on my way home?' He smiled at her. 'Life is one long rush, isn't it?'

'In four days' time? You want to know...'

She paused and he said easily, 'Yes, please, Sophie.'

The dominie was a bearded giant of a man. His wife, fair-haired and blue-eyed, offered coffee and took Sophie to see the youngest of their children, a calmly sleeping baby. 'The other three are at school. You like children?'

'Yes,' said Sophie and blushed when her companion said cheerfully,

'Of course, Rijk will want a family.'

They went round the church when they had had coffee, a severely plain edifice with whitewashed walls and small latticed windows. A number of Rijk's ancestors were buried beneath its flagstoned floor and even more in the small churchyard. His family had lived there for a very long time—centuries.

Presently they said goodbye to the dominie and his wife and took a rough little lane skirting the lake. It was very quiet there and they walked briskly, arm in arm, stopping now and then while he pointed out some thing of interest, telling her about the people and the country round them. Presently they came to the farm, a flat dwelling with a tiled and thatched roof, its huge barn at its back. 'The cows live there throughout the winter,' explained Rijk. 'Come inside with me and meet Wendel and Sierou.'

The farmer was middle-aged and powerfully built and his wife was almost as stoutly built as he was. After the first polite greetings, Rijk murmured an apology and

carried on the conversation in Friese. Dutch is bad
enough, reflected Sophie, Friese is far worse; but she
enjoyed sitting there in the vast kitchen, drinking more
coffee and listening to Rijk's quiet voice and the farmer's
rumbling replies.

They got up to go presently and walked back the way
they had come, and over lunch presently the talk had
been of a variety of matters, none of them personal.
Rijk's parents had been out too and lunched with them,
but they didn't linger over the meal since they were to
drive to Groningen.

Rijk cut through to the motorway from Drachten to
Groningen, a journey of twenty-five miles or so, which,
while quick, missed a good deal of the smaller villages.
'We shall come home through the side-roads,' he
promised her.

The city delighted her. The old houses lining the canals
were picturesque and the fifteenth-century old St
Martinkerk was magnificent. 'A pity the tower is closed
for the winter,' observed the professor. 'It is three
hundred and fifteen feet high; a splendid climb.'

'I don't like heights,' said Sophie baldly.

The university was a fairly modern building, its thou-
sands of students each wearing a coloured cap to denote
his or her faculty, and since the professor knew several
of the lecturers there they were allowed to wander around
while he patiently answered Sophie's questions.

Presently he took her to a restaurant on the Gedempte
Zuiderdiep and, while they drank their coffee, explained
the layout of the city to her. 'Of course you can see very
little of it in such a short time, but we will come again.'

She let that pass. 'Do you come to the hospitals here as well?'

'From time to time, but of course Leeuwarden is my home territory.'

Since they had finished their coffee he took her to the Prinsenhof Gardens, which even in winter were beautiful.

True to his promise, they drove back along country roads, taking a roundabout route which went through several small villages. It was already dusk but the sky was clear and there were still a few golden rays from the setting sun. The villages looked cosy and there were lighted windows in the farms they passed. There was little traffic, but they were held up from time to time by slow-moving farm carts, drawn by heavy horses. 'I like this,' said Sophie.

'So do I; this is Friesland, how I think of it when I'm away.'

Rauke, without being asked, brought in the tea-tray as soon as Sophie joined Rijk in the drawing-room. It was already five o'clock, well past the normal tea hour, but all the professor said was, 'We will dine later—there is no hurry this evening.' He said something to Rauke, who murmured a reply and went soft-footed from the room.

The tea was hot and quite strong. Sophie, when she had first arrived, had expected Earl Grey or orange pekoe—it was that kind of a house, she had decided— so it was delightful to find that the tea in the lovely old silver pot was the finest Assam. It hadn't occurred to her that the professor—a perfectionist in all he did— had taken the trouble to find out her preference. There were tiny sandwiches too and fairy cakes and a plate of biscuits which Matt was allowed to enjoy, leaning his furry bulk against his master, delighted to have them home again.

'He will miss you,' observed Sophie, sinking her nice white teeth into a fairy cake.

'Indeed, as I shall miss him. And you, Sophie, will you miss me?'

He was watching her intently and she wished that she knew how to give him a light-hearted answer which promised nothing. After all, he might be joking...

A quick glance at his impassive face made it clear that he wasn't joking; she said simply, 'Yes, I shall. I like being with you, Rijk.'

When he smiled she went on impulsively, 'And there is no need to wait...'

The door opened and his mother came into the room and Rijk got up, to all intents and purposes delighted to see her. Sophie, on the very brink of telling him that she would marry him, wondered if it was a sign of some sort to make her change her mind at the last minute.

As for the professor, there was nothing in his manner to indicate whether he regretted the interruption; his mother sat down, declaring that they had had a cup of tea an hour or more ago. 'I am very fond of your aunt Kinske, but she serves a poor cup of tea; she should speak to her cook.' She turned to Sophie. 'You enjoyed your afternoon, Sophie?'

Sophie said that yes, she had and added that she liked the villages they had driven through.

'Not at all like your own countryside, though,' Rijk's mother commented. 'I shall enjoy looking around me when we come to your wedding.'

Sophie opened her mouth to speak, caught Rijk's eye, and closed it again. He wasn't smiling, but she knew that he was amused. She went rather red and Mevrouw van Taak ter Wijsma, thinking that she was blushing for quite another reason, nodded her head in a satisfied manner.

Really, thought Sophie, they all take it for granted and I haven't even said... She remembered what she had been on the point of saying only a short time ago and made some trivial remark about the English countryside without mentioning a wedding. The professor's lips twitched and his mother thought what a nice girl Sophie was, and so exactly right for her eldest son.

The rest of the day passed pleasantly enough, but Sophie had no opportunity to speak to Rijk alone, even if she had wanted to, and, as she told herself in bed later on, she hadn't wanted to. What a good thing his mother had joined them when she had, although it would have been interesting to see what he would have done or said. He wouldn't do anything, she reflected peevishly, probably shake hands—wasn't that what friends did when they agreed to do something together? She bounced over in bed and thumped the big square pillow, feeling put out and not sure why.

She felt better in the morning; after all, she was doing what she wanted: marrying someone who shared her ideas of married life as well as a mistrust of romantic nonsense, which led only to unhappiness. She went down to breakfast with a cheerful face.

They drove to Leeuwarden later in the morning, to be joined by all five of Rijk's sisters at his parents' house, although, rather to Sophie's relief, the husbands and the children were absent. As were his brothers.

'You will see them all at the wedding,' said Mevrouw van Taak ter Wijsma in a consoling voice. She didn't appear to expect an answer, which was a good thing, for Sophie hadn't been able to think of one.

They sat over lunch; the talk was all of Christmas and the New Year and there was a good deal of sympathy for Rijk, although Tiele said, 'Next year will be different, Rijk. We'll have a marvellous family house party at your place; we can come over for the day and you can put up the rest of us.' She glanced at Sophie, 'You have brothers, haven't you, Sophie? And parents. What a splendid time we'll have...'

Sophie smiled and the professor sat back in his chair, saying nothing and looking wicked. He had put her in a very awkward position, fumed Sophie, and she would make no bones about telling him so.

Her chance came as they drove back to his home. The goodbyes had been protracted and affectionate; she had been thoroughly kissed and warmly hugged and Rijk's father had taken her hands in his and told her that Rijk would make her happy. 'I shouldn't boast of my own children, but I am sure that you will suit each other very well, and that,' he had added deliberately, 'is just as important as loving someone.'

She remembered that now, peeping at Rijk's calm profile. 'Your family seem to have made up their minds that we are to marry...'

He said easily, 'Yes, indeed. What did you think of Nanny?'

It was a successful red herring. 'Oh, she's an old darling, isn't she? A bit peppery but I can quite see why you have such an affection for her.' She paused, remembering her brief visit to the old lady, sitting cosily in the sitting-room leading from the kitchen, surrounded by dozens of photos of her charges. The room had been most comfortably furnished and Sophie had seen the bedroom leading from it.

'She wanted to be there,' explained Rijk, 'within sound of the kitchen, and of course people are popping in and out all the time so that it never gets lonely. Mother quite often has coffee with her.'

Sophie remembered that she was annoyed with him. 'You could have explained——' she began.

'No need.' He sounded placid. 'If you should decide against marrying me, then that is time enough to explain.'

'Will you be annoyed if I do that?'

'Annoyed?' He considered the question. 'Why? I thought I had made it clear that you were free to make up your mind; you are surely old and wise enough to do that.'

That nettled her. 'How well you put it,' she said peevishly.

He ignored the peevishness. 'Will you mind having your tea on your own? I still have some work to clear and we must dine early. We need to leave here around half-past seven—if we dine at half-past six? Will that suit you?'

'Yes, of course. I've only a few things left to pack.' Her ill humour had vanished; indeed, upon reflection, she wasn't quite sure why she had felt so cross in the first place.

They went on board the ferry with little time to spare, but that, she realised, was what Rijk had intended, taking Matt for a last-minute romp in the dark, cold grounds, bidding Rauke and Tyske a leisurely goodbye, and then racing smoothly through the dark evening, over the Afsluitdijk and down the motorway until they reached the Hoek with just sufficient time to go on board before the ferry sailed.

Sophie, who had watched the clock worriedly for the last fifteen minutes or so, realised that she had been anxious about nothing. Rijk was a man who knew exactly what he was doing, and she had no need to fuss. The thought was reassuring as she curled up in her bunk and went to sleep.

Her mother was waiting for them as they stopped outside her home the next morning. The door was flung wide to allow Monty and Mercury to rush out to greet them, closely followed by the lady of the house. They drank their coffee in a flurry of talk, although the professor said little.

'You must be tired,' said Mrs Blount. 'Are you sure you can't stay?'

'Quite sure, I'm afraid. I must go to St Agnes's this afternoon, but I'll come in four—no, three—days, if I may.'

'You're always welcome.' Mrs Blount gave his massive shoulder a motherly pat. 'Arthur will be back presently. You can have a nice chat while you unpack, Sophie, and I can get on with lunch.'

So Sophie had little chance to be alone with Rijk, and she wasn't sure if she was glad about that or not; certainly he gave no sign of annoyance at the lack of opportunity to be with her and presently, after lunch, when he took his leave, his placid, 'I'll see you in three days, Sophie,' and the peck she received on her cheek hardly stood for any eagerness on his part to have more of her company.

The car was barely out of sight when her mother asked, 'What have you decided, darling?' She glanced at her beautiful daughter's face. 'Perhaps you still aren't quite sure...'

Sophie sat down on the edge of the kitchen table. 'I'm sure—I think I was sure before we even went to Holland. You see, Mother, he thinks as I do; we both want a sensible, secure marriage. We like each other and we like the same things and we do get on well together. There won't be any violent feelings or quarrels. Rijk has had his share of falling in love and so have I. We shall be very happy together.'

Mrs Blount listened to this speech with an expressionless face. It sounded to her as though her dear daughter was reassuring herself, and all that nonsense about being sensible and secure. That was well enough, but no use at all without love. A good thing that Rijk loved Sophie so much that he was willing to put up with her ideas. Indeed, she suspected that he might even be encouraging them for his own ends, whatever they might be.

She said comfortably, 'Now just sit there and tell me what his home is like.'

'It's beautiful and rather grand, a long way from everywhere, although there's a village ten minutes' walk away. There's a lake close by. Mother, Rijk's a rich man—I didn't know that. Oh, I knew he was comfortably well off—I mean, he's well known internationally for his brain surgery—but I had no idea. There's a butler and a housekeeper and two maids, only he doesn't seem to be rich, because he never mentions money or his possessions. His parents have a large house in Leeuwarden and of course he has his house in London.' She cast a worried glance at her parent. 'Do you suppose it will be all right? I do like him, he's become a dear friend, and I don't care tuppence if he's without a shilling.'

'Money is nice to have, love, and I'm sure it won't make any difference to you—you're too sensible and well brought up—and someone like Rijk who has been born into it and been taught its proper place in life isn't likely to let it interfere with his way of life.' She became all at once brisk. 'I suppose you will marry quite soon? After Christmas? You will need clothes...'

'Yes, but I won't do anything until I see Rijk.'

'Of course not, dear. Now come upstairs. The boys will be home tomorrow and I've still any number of presents to tie up; do come and help me.'

The three days went quickly; there were the preparations to make for Christmas, last-minute shopping, friends calling, and the last Christmas cards to send. Sophie was in the kitchen making mince pies when Rijk arrived. She saw that he was tired and put down her rolling-pin at once and came across the kitchen to meet him.

'You've been working hard?' And then she added, 'It's nice to see you, Rijk.' She put a hand on his sleeve. 'You'll stay for lunch?'

He put a hand over hers. 'No. I must get back to the hospital as quickly as possible; I've an out-patients clinic this afternoon and a consultation. I mustn't miss the evening ferry.'

'At least have a cup of coffee—it's here, on the Aga.'

'That would be nice.' He sat down at the table and ate a mince pie, still warm from the oven. 'You're ready for Christmas?'

'Yes.' She put a mug of coffee before him and went to sit down opposite him. He took another mince pie. 'I've come for my answer, Sophie.'

'I'll marry you, Rijk, and I'll try to be a good wife—I hope I'll be able to cope...'

'Of course you will. I'll get a special licence. You would like to marry here?'

'Yes, please, and would you mind if we had a quiet wedding?'

'I should like that myself. My mother and father and Bellamy for my best man—I was his...'

'When will you be back here?'

'In two weeks' time.' He thought for a moment. 'Any day after the seventeenth of January will be fine.' He smiled suddenly at her. 'The eighteenth or nineteenth?' And when she nodded, 'I'll try to come over before then so that we can see your rector.' He put down his mug. 'I must go...'

'Where have you come from?'

'Leeds.'

'That's miles away; you must be worn out.'

'Not a bit of it.'

He came round the table and put his hands on her shoulders. 'We shall be happy, Sophie.' He bent and kissed her gently. 'And here is a token of our happiness.' He fished a small box from his pocket and opened it.

The ring inside was exquisite; sapphires and diamonds in an old-fashioned gold setting. 'My grandmother's ring; she had it from her husband's grandmother.'

He slipped it on her finger and then kissed her hand.

'Were you so sure?' asked Sophie.

'Oh, yes. *Tot ziens*, Sophie.' He had gone as unfussily as he had come, leaving her looking at the ring on her finger and wondering if other girls arranged their weddings in such a businesslike way, and all in the space of a few minutes. Of course neither she nor Rijk were hampered by sentimental ideas about getting married. She heaved a sigh and began cutting rounds of pastry and when her mother came into the kitchen she said soberly, 'He'd driven down from Leeds and he's got a full afternoon's work...'

Her mother, who had seen the professor getting into his car and been the pleased recipient of a warm hug, said cheerfully, 'Yes, dear, but I should imagine that he knows just how much he can do before he needs to rest. He's a very strong man.' She admired the ring and noted with satisfaction that Sophie was still fretting about Rijk.

'When you are married I dare say you will be able to persuade him to work a little less hard, dear. Have you fixed a date for the wedding?'

When Sophie told her she said, 'You might go and see the rector tomorrow before he gets tied up with Christmas. A quiet wedding?'

'Yes. We would both like that. Just you and Father and the boys and Rijk's mother and father and the best man—Mr Bellamy from St Anne's—they've been friends for years.'

'His sisters and brothers?' prompted Mrs Blount.

'I don't know, but I dare say they'll come—they're a close family.'

'How nice. What will you wear?'

They finished the mince pies together, arguing the merits of a winter-white outfit or a pale grey dress and jacket. It was bound to be cold and probably a grey day to boot. 'Directly Christmas is over you must go shopping.' She frowned. 'Of course the sales will be on, but you might find something.'

The boys came home presently, wished her well with brotherly affection, stated their intention of being at her wedding, and demanded to know every detail of her holiday.

'It sounds super,' commented Paul. 'We'll all come and stay and you can be the gracious lady of the house.'

'Why not?' said Sophie placidly. 'There's heaps of room and I dare say there'll be ice-skating if it gets cold enough.'

'You won't want us to visit you as soon as that,' declared Tom. 'You'll need a few weeks to be all soppy with each other.'

Sophie laughed, knowing it was expected of her. She couldn't imagine Rijk being soppy. For that matter, she had no intention of being soppy either.

She went out the next morning and bought a Dutch grammar; she must do her small best to make their marriage a success, and a good start would be to speak at least a few words of Rijk's language. There was very little time to do more than glance through its pages, what with helping around the house and helping to cook the nourishing meals her brothers constantly needed, besides entertaining various friends and acquaintances who popped in for a drink and to admire the ring. It was amazing how quickly the news had spread through the village; it wasn't until she picked up the *Telegraph* and saw the announcement of their engagement that she discovered why.

There had been no message from Rijk and although she hadn't expected one she had hoped that he might find time to phone before he left. He would be back at his home. She corrected herself; he wasn't going home, he was going straight to Schiphol. He would be in Greece now, bringing his skill to bear upon a patient with no thought of Christmas and certainly not of her.

She was mistaken. On Christmas Eve a basket of red roses, magnificent enough for a prima donna, was delivered and the card with it was in his handwriting too. He wished her a happy Christmas and was hers, Rijk.

She placed it in a prominent position in the drawing-room and looked at it every time she went into the room. He had thought of her even though he was so busy. Her lovely face took on an added sparkle and she bore her brothers' teasing remarks about red roses for love with good humour. Of course, that hadn't been Rijk's meaning; red was, after all, the colour for Christmas. It was only much later, going to bed after going to midnight service with her family, that Sophie allowed the thought which had been nagging her to be faced. Surely Rijk could have written to her or telephoned? She had made all kinds of excuses for him, but she found it hard to believe that he couldn't have scribbled a postcard before he got on the plane. The roses had been a lovely surprise, of course, but if he had had time to arrange for those he surely could have phoned her too? She lay awake wondering about it and when, at length, she slept she dreamt of him.

She hadn't been home for Christmas for several years and, despite her uneasy thoughts, she found herself soothed and reassured by the ritual of giving and receiving presents, lighting the tree, going to church again and helping her mother serve up a dinner which never varied from year to year. As she ate her turkey and Christmas pudding she wondered where she would be in a year's time—here with Rijk or in Friesland, sharing Christmas with him and his family.

'Such a pity Rijk isn't here,' observed her mother. 'I wonder what kind of a Christmas he is having?'

The professor wasn't having Christmas at all; he was undertaking a tricky piece of surgery on his patient's brain and, being a man with plenty of will-power, he hadn't allowed his thoughts to stray from this difficult task. Even when the long and complicated operation was over, he stayed within call, for the next day or two were crucial. On New Year's Eve, flying back to his home, satisfied that his work had been successful, he allowed himself to think of Sophie. He had swept her into a promise of marriage to him, but that, he was only too well aware, was only the beginning.

Rauke was waiting for him at Schiphol with an ecstatic Matt on the back seat, and he drove through the early evening back to his home, to change his clothes, wish his household a happy New Year, and then get back into his car again and drive to his parents' house, where the entire family were celebrating. He was a tired man, but no one looking at him would have seen that; he joined in the final round of drinks before midnight, piled his plate with the delicious food, and on the stroke of midnight toasted the New Year with champagne. The ceremony of kissing everyone, shaking hands and exchanging good wishes over, the professor slipped away to his father's study, and picked up the phone to dial a number.

Sophie and her family were still sitting round the fire, drinking the last of the port her father had brought up from the cellar and making sleepy plans to go to bed, when the phone rang and, since Sophie was nearest to it, she got up to answer it. Rijk's quiet voice, wishing her a happy New Year, sent a pleasant little thrill through her person; she had hoped that he might phone, but she hadn't been sure about it. She said fervently, 'Oh, Rijk,' and then, 'A happy New Year to you too. Where are you?'

'In Leeuwarden. I got back a few hours ago. I'll be with you the day after tomorrow—I'm not sure when. You'll be at home?'

'Yes, oh, yes.'

'I'll see you then. *Tot ziens*, Sophie.' He rang off and she felt vague disappointment at the brevity of his call, but it was quickly swamped at the thought of seeing him again. It surprised her that she had missed him so much.

She was in the kitchen washing her mother's best china when Mrs Broom put her head round the door.

'Yer young man's at the door, love.' She beamed at Sophie. 'Ere, give me them plates and wipe yer 'ands, mustn't keep 'im awaiting.'

Sophie thrust a valuable Wedgwood plate at Mrs Broom and dashed out of the kitchen, wiping wet, soapy hands on her pinny as she went. It was a deplorable garment, kept hanging behind the kitchen door and worn by anyone who needed it, regardless of size, but she had forgotten that.

The professor was in the hall talking to her mother, towering over her, immaculate in his cashmere overcoat and tweeds. He looked as though he might have come fresh from his valet's hands, and Sophie slithered to a halt, suddenly conscious of the apron and the fact that she hadn't bothered with her hair but tied it back with a ribbon.

The knowledge that she wasn't looking her best made her say crossly, 'I didn't expect you so soon,' and then, 'It's lovely to see you, Rijk.'

She rubbed her still wet hands on the apron. 'I was just washing the best china...'

The professor's eyes gleamed beneath their lids. 'I like the hair,' he said and bent to kiss her. 'Shall I come and help you with the plates?'

'No, of course not.' She smiled, her good humour restored, feeling comfortable with him just as friends should with each other. 'I'll fetch the coffee—did you come over on the night ferry?'

'Yes. I've a case this afternoon at St Agnes's but I wondered if we might go and see your parson this morning? I'll come back this evening and we'll go out to dinner; there is a good deal to discuss.'

She nodded. 'Yes. Are you going to be in England for a while?'

'I'm afraid not. Two or three days. I've a good deal of work waiting for me and I'd like to get it done before the wedding.'

'Yes, of course.' They went into the sitting-room, where her mother had prudently retired, and presently, over coffee which that lady brought, the conversation turned to the wedding.

'A quiet one?' her mother asked and went on, 'Just a handful of people—we can all come back here for lunch afterwards if you would like that. I dare say you'll want to be off somewhere or other.'

'We shall catch the night ferry to Holland; I can spare only a couple of days.'

'Well, let me know what you arrange between you,' said Mrs Blount comfortably, 'and I'll fit in.' She spoke cheerfully; like all mothers she would have liked to see her beautiful daughter swanning down the aisle in white satin and her own wedding veil, which she had kept so carefully for just such an occasion; it might have comforted her if she had known that Sophie had had a fleeting regret that the white satin and veil weren't for her. Only for a moment, however; a romantic wedding would have been ridiculous in their case. All the same, she would find something suitable for a bride, however modest the wedding...

Her father and Tom came in presently and she slipped away to take great pains with her face and hair and present herself in a quilted jacket and woolly gloves, ready to go to the rectory with Rijk.

They walked there, talking idly about this and that, very much at ease with each other, and when they reached the rectory the professor, while giving the appearance of asking Sophie's opinion about dates and times, had everything arranged exactly as he had planned it. The wedding was to be at eleven o'clock in the morning in two weeks' time by special licence; it was to be a quiet ceremony. As they would be leaving for Holland that same day they were both most grateful to the rector for arranging to marry them at rather short notice.

'Delighted, delighted,' observed the old man, 'and I trust that I may have the happy task of christening your children.'

Sophie smiled, murmured and avoided Rijk's eye, and was a little surprised to hear his agreement, uttered in a grave voice, although she felt he meant it. Of course, she told herself, he didn't want to hurt the rector's feelings. That was the one doubt she had about their marriage; she liked children and she rather thought that Rijk did too, but if they kept to their agreement and lived the life he had envisaged there wouldn't be any. Of course, perhaps later on... In the meantime, she told herself, they would share a very pleasant life together without heartbreak and the pitfalls of falling in love. She walked back with Rijk, quite content with her future.

He left shortly after they got back with the reminder that he would be back in the early evening. As he got into the car he asked her, 'Have you any preference as to where we should go?'

'Must it be a restaurant?' she asked diffidently. 'Would it be a bother to Percy and Mrs Wiffen if we dined at your house?'

She was rewarded by his pleased look. 'No bother at all; they're all agog at the idea of a wedding and I'm sure they're longing to see the bride again.' He kissed her cheek lightly, got into the car, and drove off, leaving her to go into the house and go through her wardrobe for something suitable to wear. The brown velvet skirt and ivory silk blouse with the frilled collar would do nicely...

The evening was a great success; Percy and Mrs Wiffen had presented them with a delicious meal and afterwards they had sat in the drawing-room by the fire, talking. Waking in the night, Sophie had been unable to remember what they had talked about, only the satisfying memory of it. It was only when she woke again just as it was getting light that she knew without any doubt at all that she had fallen in love with Rijk.

CHAPTER SEVEN

SOPHIE got up and dressed, although it was still early; to lie in bed was quite impossible. She dragged on an old raincoat, tied a scarf over her hair, pulled on her wellies, and went quietly out of the house.

Montgomery and Mercury, delighted at the prospect of a walk so early in the day, slid through the back door after her, and she was glad of their company.

It was drizzling with a cold rain and the wind was bitter, but she really hadn't noticed either. 'Now I'm in a pickle, aren't I?' she asked them. 'Must I say that I've changed my mind or shall I go ahead and marry him and then pretend for the rest of my days that I've nothing but friendly feelings towards him?'

Mercury gave a sympathetic yelp and Montgomery huffed deep in his throat.

'The thing is,' went on Sophie, intent on getting things straight in her head, 'is it better never to see him again or marry him and never let him know that I love him?' She added in a shaky little voice, 'He's the one, you see. I know that now; I can't think why I didn't discover it earlier. No one else really matters. He does like me, we get on so well together—like old friends, if you see what I mean—and I don't think I could bear never to see him again...'

She stopped in the middle of the muddy lane and the dogs stopped with her, looking at her with sympathetic eyes. 'I'm going to marry him,' she told them briskly. 'Half a loaf is very much better than no bread.'

She turned for home, her mind made up, and feeling relieved, so that when, over breakfast, her mother broached the subject of buying clothes she agreed that the sooner she did some shopping the better.

'And I wonder how many of Rijk's family are coming to the wedding?' her mother mused. 'Should I invite them?' She didn't wait for an answer. 'I'll write a note to his mother and invite any member of the family who might wish to come.' She began to reckon on her fingers. 'There will be nine of them if they all come, and I haven't counted the husbands...'

'They won't come to the wedding,' said Sophie. 'Just his mother and father and perhaps a brother or sister. He told me that there will be a big family gathering when we get back to Friesland.'

'Then I'll cater for about twenty to be on the safe side. I must see about the wedding-cake this morning. When will you go shopping, love?'

'Tomorrow; I don't need much...'

'No, dear, perhaps not, but one or two good outfits besides your wedding clothes.'

Sophie gave her mother a dreamy look, her head full of Rijk. 'Winter-white if I can find it, a coat and dress, and I'll have to buy a hat.'

Her mother gave her a thoughtful look; if she hadn't known better she would have said that the dear girl was in love, her head in the clouds and her wits addled.

'That would be very nice,' she said in a matter-of-fact voice. 'Will you be seeing Rijk before the wedding?'

'No, he goes back to Holland tomorrow. He wants to clear up as much as possible before we are married.'

She went up to London the next morning. Her father drove her into Chipping Ongar and put her on the London train with instructions to spend the cheque he had given her, and if she needed more money she had only to ask for it. There was money in her own bank account too; if she wanted to she could be wildly extravagant. Why not? she reflected. It was her wedding and she wanted Rijk to be proud of her.

She avoided the big stores where the sales were in full swing; there were several boutiques where, even if they had sales, they would have something to suit her tucked away.

By late afternoon she was tired, hungry and triumphant. She also had a charming outfit for the wedding, a winter-white dress and long loose coat to match it in a fine woollen material. Even with a few pounds taken off as a concession to the sales, the price had been horrific, but, as the owner of the boutique had said, it was an outfit which could be worn repeatedly and not lose its chic. There was a hat to go with it too, a confection of velvet and feathers, faintly pink-tipped.

'A wedding outfit?' murmured the saleslady, who had seen Sophie's ring.

'Well, yes—a very quiet wedding...'

'Exactly suitable and very elegant. You have a splendid figure, if I may say so, madam. I expect you have already bought a good deal, but I do have a jersey suit—so suitable for this time of year. It is your size and I would be pleased to make a reduction on its price.'

A jersey suit would be useful, Sophie had reflected, and, since it was a perfect fit and a mixture of blues and greens which suited her dark hair and eyes, she bought that too.

She had snatched a hasty lunch then before going in search of something for the evening. Rijk lived in some style; certainly there would be at least one dance or dinner. This time she found exactly what she wanted— a dress with a full long skirt, the bodice square-necked and with tiny sleeves. It was in almond-pink chiffon and suitable, she hoped, for an eminent surgeon's wife, and since she still had some money in her purse she bought a brown and gold brocade top, high-necked and long-sleeved; it would go well with her brown velvet skirt... Marks and Spencer provided her with new undies and, well pleased with her purchases, she went back home.

It had been a lovely day and beneath the excitement of buying new clothes was the knowledge that she loved Rijk, and that was exciting too, so that when he phoned later that evening she was for the moment bereft of words.

In answer to his quiet 'Sophie?' she said breathlessly, 'Rijk, where are you?'

'At Eernewoude. What have you done with your day?'

'I bought a wedding-dress... Will you be there until you come back here?'

'No, four or five days here and then a quick trip to Brussels to see a patient and then here again until I leave for England. You may not hear from me for a day or two...'

'That's all right,' said Sophie. She wanted him to phone her every day—twice a day if possible—just to hear his voice, but on no account must he ever know that. 'You don't need to bother; we'll see to everything.'

She wasn't sure, but it sounded as though he had laughed before he said goodbye.

There was plenty to keep her occupied at home; her mother had sent invitations to Rijk's family and was happily immersed in preparations for the wedding breakfast. 'Something simple,' she declared, 'if you have to leave for the ferry.' She paused. 'But doesn't that go at night? Rijk said he would want to leave directly after we have had lunch.'

'Perhaps he wants to call at his London house,' suggested Sophie.

'Probably.' Her mother frowned. 'Smoked salmon and those little cheese puffs, baby sausage rolls and tiny quiches—the kind you can hold in your hand without them going crumbly—and the cake, of course...'

Sophie said, 'Yes, Mother,' in a dreamy voice. As far as she was concerned they could chew cardboard just as long as she and Rijk were safely married. It would take time, she reflected, to get him to fall in love with her. She knew that she was a lovely girl and, while not in the least bit conceited, she knew that it was an asset. Rijk thought of her as a friend; all she had to do was to get him to see her in a different light... as an attractive woman as well as a practical young woman who understood his work and was prepared to take second place to it in his life.

She thought about it a good deal during the next few days. The thing was to make him see her in a new light. She still hadn't planned a course of action by the time he returned, and it was hard to behave as she always had done, to greet him with the friendly pleasure he expected and answer his questions about their wedding in a matter-of-fact voice.

His parents and two of his sisters had travelled over at the same time, driven their own car, and gone straight to his London home; only he had driven on to see her and make sure that everything was in train for the next day.

'Loewert and Iwert are flying over this evening—Bellamy will bring them down in the morning. That makes seven on my side. How many have you?'

They were sitting in the kitchen drinking coffee, and she tried not to look at him too often; just having him there, close to her, was sending her heart thumping at her ribs. She told herself silently not to be silly. 'Well, there's Mother and Father and the boys—that's five—and me, of course, and you... That's fourteen. The rector and his wife will come to lunch—it's a buffet.' She cast him a quick look. 'We weren't sure when you would want to leave.'

'I thought we might have dinner at home, just the two of us, before we go to the ferry.'

She nodded agreement. 'Mother would love everyone to stay for tea and supper; it would be nice if everyone got to know everyone else.' She added, 'I forgot Mr Bellamy...'

'He'll have to go back soon after we leave.'

The professor got up from his chair opposite her and came and sat on the corner of the table, close to her. 'No doubts?' he asked softly.

She gave him a direct look. 'None at all,' she told him clearly.

He bent and kissed her. 'Nor I. Shall we go for a walk? I'm going back after lunch; I'm sure you want to wash your hair or whatever women do before they get married.'

Sophie laughed. 'Well, as a matter of fact, I do have to do that—however did you know?'

'Remember that I have five sisters.' He pulled her to her feet. 'Get a coat and I'll find your mother.' He glanced at his watch. 'Is lunch at one o'clock? Then we have all of two hours.'

It was a cold morning, but there was a watery sun and they walked briskly.

'Tell me about your trip to Greece,' said Sophie. 'Was the op successful?'

She listened with real interest, understanding what he was talking about and asking sensible questions from time to time, and the professor paused in the middle of a particularly complicated explanation to say, 'What a pleasure it is to be able to talk about my work to someone who understands me. It is said that one shouldn't take one's work home with one, but how satisfactory it will be to come home and mull over my work without fear of boring you.'

'You would never bore me,' said Sophie and went bright pink because she had sounded a bit too fervent. She wasn't looking at him and didn't see his slow smile. She added quickly, 'Don't forget that I've been nursing for a long time.'

'Shall you miss it?' he asked casually. 'Life at Eernewoude is quiet...'

'I shall like that and there will be so much to keep me busy—I must learn to speak Dutch and understand it, and there's Matt and getting to know everyone in the village and your family.'

'We shall entertain too, Sophie. I have many friends and there is a surprisingly brisk social life. And when we are married I suspect it will be even brisker.'

'You will like that?'

'Not very much. I shall rely on you to fend off all but my closest friends.'

'You'll have to give me a list,' said Sophie, 'and I'll do my best.'

The professor went again after lunch, but not before he had given Sophie his wedding gift—diamond and sapphire earrings, the sapphires surrounded by diamonds, hanging from diamond-studded pendants. She put them on, struck dumb with their beauty. 'They're magnificent,' she told him. 'Thank you, Rijk, I'll wear them tomorrow...' She reached up to kiss his cheek. 'I can't give you diamonds and sapphires, can I? Only a wedding-ring...'

'Which I shall wear with pride.'

Sophie was up early on her wedding-day; she had slept well, but once awake there was no point in lying in bed—she was too excited. She was happy too and at the same time apprehensive. It would be heaven to be with Rijk each and every day, but supposing, just supposing he found her boring or, worse, fell in love with another woman? A beautiful face wasn't enough; she knew that... She crept down to the kitchen and made herself some tea and sat drinking it by the Aga with the dogs on either side of her. Soothed by the warmth and the ordinary action, she went back upstairs to bath and presently have an early breakfast in her dressing-gown.

Even if she had wanted to brood she had no chance; her brothers saw to that until her mother bustled her back to her room to dress.

'Mother, there's heaps of time,' she protested.

'You must dress and then sit quietly and compose yourself,' said her parent. 'Anyhow, I want everyone out of the way. Mrs Broom will be here with her daughter in a few minutes and I must make sure that everything is ready in the drawing-room.'

So Sophie dressed and went to sit in her window; she could see the church spire above the trees. In less than an hour she would be beneath it, getting married. She wondered what Rijk was doing; supposing he got held up on the way—an accident, roads up for repair, a puncture? She was glad when her mother came in to ask her advice as to the exact angle of her new hat. They studied it together in the looking-glass. 'Very mother-of-the-bride,' said Sophie. 'You do look nice, Mother, dear.'

'Will Rijk's mother look nice too?'

'I'm sure she will—she looks a bit fierce but she isn't. I think you'll like each other.'

The house was quiet once her mother and brothers had gone; she sat in the drawing-room with her father, waiting for the hired limousine to take them to the church. In a few hours she would have left home, she reflected, and took comfort from the thought that Rijk had said that she might come over to England whenever he did and see her family. He was a kind man, she mused, as well as a close friend. And, of course, a husband.

The car came and they got in and were driven the short distance to the church, and, Sophie being Sophie, there was no nonsense about being late—it was striking eleven o'clock as, holding the small, exquisite bouquet Rijk had sent her, and her arm tucked in her father's, she walked down the aisle.

For a quiet wedding the church was remarkably full. The village, delighted to have a dull winter day enlivened by such an event, had turned out in force, crowding the pews behind Sophie's family and Rijk's parents, two of his sisters and his brothers, sitting on the other side of the aisle. But she barely glanced at them; Rijk was there, waiting for her, his massive bulk reassuring even though he didn't turn to look at her. Only when they were standing beside him did he turn and smile into her eyes for a moment before the service began.

She became aware then that there was music and the choir and flowers. She wondered who had arranged that and then made herself listen to the rector's old voice and presently, obediently following his quavering tones, promising to love, honour and obey...

They went out of the church arm in arm and she smiled vaguely from side to side, feeling as though she were in a dream, and at the church door they had to pause for a moment while someone took photos, and then everyone else crowded round them and she was being kissed and everyone was talking at once.

In the Bentley, beside Rijk, she asked, 'Who arranged for the choir and the organ and all those lovely flowers?'

'I did. I wanted you to have a fitting background, Sophie.'

'Thank you, it was all so—so... I don't know the right word, but do you know what I mean?'

'Yes. I think I do. You look very beautiful, my dear.'

'Oh, thank you.' She glanced sideways at him; his grey suit was magnificently cut, his tie a rich silk in a darker shade, a white carnation in his buttonhole; he was the epitome of a well dressed man. 'You look awfully nice yourself.'

He dropped a hand on her knee. 'A well suited couple, are we not?'

The wedding breakfast was a triumph. Mrs Blount glowed with pride. She had had to get caterers in, of course, but a good deal of it she had seen to herself. She beamed around her; Sophie looked marvellous, so did Rijk, and she and his mother had taken to each other immediately. She had found his father a little daunting to start with, but then she had seen the twinkle in his eyes—the same eyes as his son. After all, he was only an older edition of Rijk. His sisters and brothers were friendly too and there was no worry about understanding them; their English was as good as hers. She went and sat down by Rijk's mother and that lady patted her arm. 'This is a delightful occasion—we can be proud of our new son and daughter, can we not? As soon as they are settled in you must all come over and stay with us—we have plenty of room for the boys and even if we hadn't there are so many of us that there is always a room for anyone who cares to come and stay.'

'You're very kind,' said Mrs Blount and added, 'I'm very fond of Rijk—we all are. He—he just sort of fitted in from the moment he came to see us.' The two ladies smiled mistily at each other and Mrs Blount said, 'I think it is time to cut the cake; they want to be off by two o'clock.'

They drove away in a shower of confetti, still in their wedding clothes, for they were to change at the London house.

'Warm enough?' asked Rijk.

'Yes, thank you. Won't your family want to come to the London house this evening?'

'After we have gone—Father has arranged for everyone to dine at Ingatestone...'

'The Heybridge Moat House?'

'That's the one. They can discuss the wedding at their ease; it won't matter how late they are. He's arranged for a car for Loewert and Iwert and he'll drive Mother and the girls back himself. He phoned your father this morning...'

'How very kind and thoughtful of him.' She looked out of the window at the wintry fields. 'What time do we have to leave London?'

'About eight o'clock; we'll dine first.' He smiled down at her. 'I enjoyed our wedding, did you?'

She realised with some surprise that she had. She had expected it to be a kind of dream in which she wouldn't feel quite real, but it had been real enough and she had felt happy... 'Yes, I did. I've heard people say that they couldn't remember their wedding clearly, but I can remember every word.'

She didn't say any more; the wish to tell him that she loved him was so strong that she had to clench her teeth, and presently he asked, 'Tired? We'll soon be home.'

She hurried to tell him that she wasn't in the least tired, that it was excitement. 'So much has happened today—it was so nice having your people here, and our mothers took to each other at once, didn't they?'

She embarked on a rather pointless conversation about the wedding and felt relief when they reached the outskirts of London and he was forced to slow down and give his whole attention to the traffic.

Percy opened the door with a flourish as the professor stopped before his house. 'Heartiest congrats, guv, and you, madam. All the best and lots of little 'uns. This is an 'appy day and no mistake.'

'Why, thank you, Percy.' The professor sounded at his most placid and Sophie, doing her best to follow his example, shook Percy's hand and thanked him.

'Well, now. There's champagne in the drawing-room and Mrs Wiffen 'as bust her stays over yer dinner.' Percy beamed at them as he took Sophie's coat.

'If I may say so, madam, you look smashing. I'll fetch in the luggage in half a mo'—you'll want to change before you leave.'

He urged them into the drawing-room, softly lighted and decked with enough flowers to stock a florist's shop. 'Me and Mrs Wiffen thought as 'ow it'd be nice ter 'ave a few flowers,' explained Percy, and something in his voice sent Sophie across the room to take his hand in hers.

'Percy, how kind of you both, and the room looks beautiful. It's such a lovely surprise; how I wish we could take them all with us to Holland.'

'Well, there is that... P'raps yer could take a small bunch wiv yer?'

'I most certainly shall. I've never seen such a wonderful display. Thank you and Mrs Wiffen; you couldn't have pleased us more, could they, Rijk?'

The professor, thus addressed, made haste to add his appreciation to Sophie's, and Percy, looking pleased with himself, went away, back to the kitchen to tell Mrs Wiffen that the newly wed pair looked a treat and no mistake. 'A bit of all right is the missus and that's for sure,' he pronounced.

Sophie sat by the fire in the steel grate and drank the champagne which Rijk had poured for her. Rijk sat down and with a word of excuse became immersed in a pile of letters beside his chair.

'It looks as though I shall have to come back here in about six weeks' time.' He glanced at her, smiling. 'You might come too if you wish to see your parents. I shall have to go to Denmark too very shortly, just to operate; I dare say you will find plenty to do at home...'

She saw that she wasn't to be allowed to interfere with his work in any way. She agreed serenely and drank her champagne.

Mrs Wiffen had excelled herself: crab mousse, surrounded by a sauce of her own invention, followed by grilled Dover sole with tiny potatoes and braised celery in a cheese sauce and rounded off by a confection of fresh pineapple and meringue. They drank their coffee at the table and Sophie said, diffidently, 'Would you mind if I went to the kitchen and thanked Mrs Wiffen? She has gone to a great deal of trouble...'

Rijk got up as she did. 'I'll come with you.'

Mrs Wiffen, treated to a sight of the bride's outfit, was almost tearful. 'I'm sure we so wish you happiness, madam, and you, sir. I 'opes you'll be back soon to sample some more of my cooking.'

'I look forward to that,' said Sophie. 'The professor often comes here and I shall come with him.'

She went upstairs presently to a charming bedroom, its satinwood furniture gleaming in the soft pink glow of the shaded lamps, the bedspread and curtains in quilted pastel chintz. Someone had unpacked her case and her travelling clothes were lying ready. She got out of her wedding outfit, folded it carefully in tissue paper, and packed it. There was really no point in taking it with her, but to leave it behind was unthinkable...

Presently, dressed for the journey, she went downstairs again in the jersey suit and her winter coat. It was a cold night and it might be even colder in Holland; she had prudently stuffed a scarf and thick gloves in her pockets.

Rijk, in tweeds and his cashmere overcoat, was waiting for her in the hall, talking to Mrs Wiffen and Percy.

'Oh, have I kept you waiting?' Sophie hurried forward to be reassured by Rijk's placid,

'Not at all, my dear! You are most punctual and we have plenty of time.'

She made her goodbyes, taking the little bouquet of flowers which Percy offered her. 'I'll put them in water the moment we arrive,' she told him, 'to remind me of your beautiful decorations for us this evening.'

'Be seein' you,' said Percy cheerfully, and he and Mrs Wiffen waved from the door as Rijk drove away.

It had been cold in London; it seemed to Sophie as they drove away from the Hoek the next morning very early that it was a great deal colder in Holland. The Bentley was warm, though, and they stopped presently for coffee at a small café by the motorway.

Sophie bit into a *kaas broodje*. 'How long a holiday have you got?' she asked.

'I've several patients to see in two days' time, then I shall be in Amsterdam for a few days; after that I shall be home for some time...'

He spoke casually, but his eyes were on her face.

Sophie summoned an interested smile. 'Oh, yes, you must have a marvellous secretary keeping tabs on your appointments.' She reflected that it was only what she had expected after all. He was no lovesick bridegroom and she must take care not to dwindle into a lovesick bride. If she hadn't fallen in love with him she would have been quite content with his answer.

They drove on presently, going north along the east side of the Ijsselmeer, skirting Utrecht and then on to Meppel and Drachten. The short day was drawing to its close as they turned in between the gates of his home. They had stopped a few miles before Zwolle and had their lunch at a small restaurant tucked away from the main road. They had had the typical Dutch lunch—*koffietafel*—omelette, a basket of rolls and bread, cheese and cold meats and as much coffee as they could drink. The restaurant was fairly full and pleasantly warm and Sophie left it reluctantly to go back outside into the grey day, but once she was in the car beside Rijk her spirits rose again. They were starting this, their married life, together and she had every intention of making a success of it—and that was the least of it; surely, with a little encouragement on her part, he might, in time, fall in love with her...

They received a warm welcome, with Matt racing out of the house to lean against them, and Rauke, Tyske and the two maids were waiting in the porch despite the cold.

There was tea waiting for them, and Sophie, bidden to hurry down from her room as quickly as possible, did so to find Rijk sitting in his great wing-chair by the fire, sorting through a pile of letters. He got up as she went in and put the letters down, and she said at once, 'Do read your post; there may be something important,' and sat down beside the tea-tray and poured the tea, feeling unreasonably hurt when he did so. It was, after all, only yesterday that they had married.

She drank her tea and ate the little cakes Tyske had made and tried to look as relaxed as Rijk, sitting there going through his correspondence as though they had been married for years... Presently she went back to her lovely room to find that her things had been unpacked and put away in the wall closet and the tallboy drawers. There was nothing for her to do but bath and change into the brown velvet skirt and one of the silk tops to go with it. That done, she went and sat by the window and looked out on to the dark grounds around the house, the darkness pierced by the light streaming from its many windows. She could hear Matt barking and presently saw him dashing across the lawns below, followed by Rijk, who looked up and, when he saw her, waved.

She went downstairs then and found him waiting for her. 'I dare say you're tired,' he observed kindly. 'I usually dine at eight o'clock when I'm here, but I asked Rauke to serve us earlier this evening. Come and sit down and have a drink first. Is your room quite comfortable? If there is anything that you need you have only to ask.'

She had the strange feeling that she was a guest in his house as she assured him that she had everything that she could possibly want, glad of Matt's attentions as she sat down and then took the glass offered to her. Presently, she felt better; Rijk was completely at ease, much as though they had been married for years and sitting there chatting over drinks was something they had done forever...

However matter-of-fact Rijk was over their home-coming, Rauke and Tyske had seen to it that it should be marked in an appropriate manner. The dining-table, decked with white damask, gleamed with silver and crystal, and the arrangement of flowers at its centre was decidedly bridal: white roses and freesias, pale pink tulips and lilies of the valley and blue hyacinths; they smelled delicious. The professor, who had conferred with Rauke over this, their first dinner as a married couple in their own home, watched Sophie's face and was content at the look of surprised delight upon it.

The dinner itself was delicious: watercress soup, lobster thermidor with a potato salad and dishes of vegetables followed by a lemon sorbet and a spectacular *bombe glacée*. They ate unhurriedly and Sophie found her initial vague disappointment melting under her husband's undemanding conversation, and presently, when they went back to the drawing-room to have their coffee by the fire, she said, 'What a nice homecoming, and how beautifully Rauke and Tyske look after you.'

'They will look after you just as well, Sophie. In a few days, when you feel at your ease here, Tyske will take you round the house—she is most anxious to inspect the household linen and the kitchen cupboards with you. Rauke will translate for you, but I'm sure that within a short time you'll be able to manage on your own. I dare say you would like some Dutch lessons? I'll see to that for you. Tomorrow we will go and see those of the family who were not at the wedding, and if you like to come to Leeuwarden with me on the following day...? I'll show you where the hospital is and you had better meet the head porter so that if you should need me they can arrange for you to see me at once.'

She agreed quietly; life was going to be strange for a time, but she would learn quickly. She suspected that he expected her to have her own interests when he was away, and she would have to be careful not to infringe upon his life but just to be there when he wanted her company. That would all be altered, she told herself, but it might take time. He had got what he wanted, the kind of wife and marriage he wanted—it was up to her to change his mind for him.

She glanced across at him, loving very much every line of his face, longing to shout her feelings out loud; instead, after a suitable time had elapsed, she wished him a friendly goodnight and took herself off to bed. He had opened the door for her and kissed the top of her head as she passed him, an action she treasured as she lay in bed, considering the future.

They were to have lunch with his three sisters who hadn't been at the wedding. Siska, the eldest of them, welcomed them to her house and Sophie found all three of them there. They hugged Rijk and kissed her with warmth and wanted to know everything there was to tell about the wedding. 'We would have loved to have come,' said Siska, 'but you knew about the measles, didn't you? When Mother and Father are back and the rest of us as well, we shall have a family party. There are many uncles and aunts and cousins all wishing to meet you.'

Sophie, having assured her sisters-in-law that she had had the measles, was taken to visit her spotty little nephews and nieces. Later, going back home with Rijk, she said, 'What a nice family you have, Rijk; I do like them.'

'They like you too. You will see a good deal of them, you know.'

Breakfast was to be early in the morning since Rijk was due at the hospital by nine o'clock. Sophie, well wrapped against the chilly morning, drove with him to Leeuwarden, was shown where the hospital was, told at what time to be there in the afternoon, given a roll of notes, and told to go and enjoy herself, which, rather to her surprise, she did. There was plenty to see and she spent a long time choosing wool. Knitting was something she had never had much time for; but now there was the chance to get expert at it. She bought canvas and tapestry wools too and several paperbacks as well as a notebook and a useful book entitled *A guide to Dutch for the tourist*. Even a smattering of that language would be useful.

Rijk went to Amsterdam the following day, leaving while it was still dark, and, since he wouldn't be home again until early evening, Sophie filled the hours by inspecting cupboards of linen—enough to last forever, she considered—and more vast cupboards in the kitchen and the pantry, filled with china and glass, and then, lastly, she was shown the safe where the family silver was kept. By the time Rijk got home she was beginning to feel that she was a married woman with a home to run.

The next day she went to the kitchen and sat down at the table there with Tyske while Rauke translated his wife's detailed account of just how the house was run. She enjoyed that; it was a lived-in room and something on the massive Aga smelled delicious. There was a cat and kittens too in a basket before the stove and Matt sitting beside her, watching her lovingly with his yellow eyes.

Rijk was tired when he got home, but not too tired to tell her of his day, and she made a good listener, sitting there with her knitting, asking all the right questions in a quiet voice. Halfway through an account of a patient's treatment he paused to say, 'Did I ever tell you what a restful girl you are, Sophie? I enjoy coming home and finding you here, knowing that I can talk to you and that you will listen intelligently and we are good friends enough for you to tell me when I begin to bore you.'

'Oh, I'll do that,' she assured him, making her voice briskly friendly, 'but it's not likely.'

'I must arrange for you to meet some of my friends so that they may be your friends too, and you must come to the hospital...' He smiled suddenly. 'No one expects us to be very social for a week or two.'

She summoned a smile in return. She hoped it looked like an understanding smile between friends.

Rijk finished at Amsterdam and, although he went to Leeuwarden or Groningen each day, she saw more of him. They walked together in the early mornings with Matt and, although he spent most of the evening in his study, at least he was in the house. Sophie began to feel cautiously happy.

It was several days after he had come back from Amsterdam that she decided to go to Leeuwarden. Rauke was taking the Land Rover in to fetch groceries and she went with him, assuring him that she would go to the hospital and return home with the professor. She spent the early afternoon searching for the extra wools and needles she would need for her tapestry and then made her way to the hospital, nicely in time to meet Rijk.

She was opposite the hospital forecourt, waiting for a lull in the traffic, when she saw him coming out of the entrance. He wasn't alone; a tall, slender woman was beside him, laughing up at him, and he was holding her arm as they walked towards the Bentley. Sophie shut her eyes and then opened them again; they hadn't deceived her. The pair of them were in the car and Rijk swiftly drove it out of the forecourt; moreover, he was going in the opposite direction from his home...

CHAPTER EIGHT

SOPHIE watched the tail-lights of the Bentley disappear, oblivious of the impatient people jostling her as they hurried past her. Who was the woman Rijk was with and where were they going? It was plain that they knew each other. Rijk had been laughing... Sophie ground her splendid teeth and looked around for a policeman.

Yes, he told her, holding up the traffic while he explained where the bus depot was, there would certainly be a bus to Grouw, but she would need to hurry. She thanked him nicely from a white face and hurried through the streets and found the bus, already full, on the point of leaving. Once on it, jammed between two old men with baskets of eels and smelling strongly of fish, she pondered what she would do when she got to Grouw. Eernewoude was still some miles further at the end of a secondary road which meandered round the lake. She would have to hire a taxi... One of the old men spoke to her and she dredged up her few words of Dutch—*'Ik ben Engels'*—and gave him a smile, and he broke into instant speech. Not even Dutch, she thought despairingly, but Friese, which sounded even more unintelligible than Dutch. There was a stirring in the bus, for he had a loud voice, and someone said, 'English—Professor van Taak ter Wijsma's wife, yes?'

'Yes,' said Sophie, feeling awkward.

'On a bus?' said the same voice. 'You have no car? You are alone?' The owner of the voice sounded quite shocked. 'The professor is not allowing that?'

Of course, in this sparsely populated part of Friesland, he would be known, at least by name. She said clearly, 'I was to go home with him, but I have missed him in Leeuwarden. He will fetch me in Grouw.

'That's not likely,' she murmured to herself, listening to the satisfied chat around her.

The bus stopped frequently, presumably to suit the wishes of the passengers getting on and off in the dark night. There were few villages, for the bus was travelling along a country lane, away from the main road, but there would be farms. Indeed, when she bent to peer out of a window she could see a light here and there away from the road. It looked lonely country and she wished that she was at home, sitting by the fire, working away at her tapestry. The two old men were still on either side of her, talking across her as though she weren't there, and she allowed her thoughts to wander. Where was Rijk? she wondered. And if she asked him when she got home would he tell her?

The bus rattled to a halt in Grouw and she got out last of all, her ears ringing with the chorus of *'Dag'* from her companions on the journey. Now to find a taxi... She turned round to get her bearings and found Rijk right behind her.

Surprise took her breath, but only for a moment. She said in a rush, 'I went into Leeuwarden with Rauke and I meant to meet you at the hospital, but they said you'd already left, so I caught a bus...'

He had a hand on her arm. 'I left early. I'm sorry you had this long, cold ride.' He was walking her across to the Bentley.

'I enjoyed it. Everyone talked and I didn't understand any of it. How did you know that I would be on the bus?'

'Rauke had expected you to be with me. You're a sensible girl; I knew you would get yourself back, and this was the last bus to Grouw. I got back into the car and drove over.'

'I was going to get a taxi.'

The car was blissfully warm and Matt's breath was hot on the back of her neck. Seated comfortably, she was waiting for him to tell her why he had left with that girl, but it was evident that he wasn't going to, even though she stayed silent so that he had the chance to do so. Instead he observed casually that the following week there was to be a reception at the hospital in their honour. 'And Mother phoned today; they are back and there is to be a family dinner within the next week or so. You will enjoy that, will you not, Sophie? Perhaps life is a little dull for you here.'

'Dull? Certainly not. The days aren't long enough— not that I do anything useful, but I'm always busy.'

'I'm glad you are happy here. I hear that cold weather is expected, with snow, which means that we shall be able to skate.'

'I can't...'

He stopped the car in front of the house and turned to look at her. 'I'll teach you; it's splendid exercise— the children have days off from school and they light up the canals.'

She forced herself to answer with a show of enthusiasm, hoping against hope that he would explain. He didn't, however. They reached home and he got out and helped her from the car and over the icy steps to the door. He nodded to Rauke as they went inside but made no move to take off his coat.

'I've a meeting in Leeuwarden this evening; shall you mind dining alone? I shall probably be back late.'

She minded very much but she wasn't going to say so. 'What about your dinner?'

'Oh, we have sandwiches and coffee and Rauke will leave something for me in the kitchen. Don't wait up, my dear.' He dropped a casual kiss on her cheek. 'I'll see you in the morning.'

He took Matt with him so that she had no company as she dined and afterwards, sitting by the fire, savagely poking her needle in and out of her tapestry work.

She went to bed early because he had made it clear that he didn't expect to see her when he got home, and she lay awake until she heard the car whisper to a halt below her window and presently his quiet footsteps in the house.

'I've made a mess of things,' muttered Sophie, weeping into her pillow.

In the morning at the breakfast-table she was bright and brisk, making a brief reference to his meeting without waiting for an answer. He asked her then what she was going to do with her day, and she told him that she intended to explore the attics, take Matt for a walk, and be home in time for Loewert, who had phoned to say that he would call.

'I dare say he'll stay for dinner,' she observed, and Rijk looked surprised.

'By all means; I should be home in good time this evening.'

'How nice,' said Sophie sweetly. She met his thoughtful look with a smile. 'Do you suppose it will snow today?'

'Very likely. Don't go near the lake; it's beginning to freeze over, but it won't be safe for several days.' He got up from the table and offered her a handful of envelopes. 'Invitations—will you look through them? And we'll decide what to do about them.'

'Yes, of course.' She gave him an overbright smile. 'Don't do too much.'

Loewert arrived just before lunch. 'I'm playing truant,' he told her happily. 'I've exams at the end of the week and I thought a day away from my books might help.'

'What exams are they?' She led him into the drawing-room and they sat down before the fire with the coffee-tray between them.

'Ear, nose and throat and gynae.'

She passed him his cup and watched him spoon sugar with a lavish hand.

'You think you'll pass?'

He grinned and she thought with a little leap of her heart that Rijk must have looked like that when he was younger. 'I hope I will. With old Rijk as an example, what else can I do? He's the one with the brains, of course, though he'd give me a good thump if he heard me saying that.'

He looked at Sophie, quite serious for a moment. 'He's a splendid fellow, you know—but of course you do;

you're married to him.' He passed his cup for more coffee and took another biscuit. 'We were beginning to think that he would never find himself a wife, and then you turned up, an answer to our prayers—a beautiful angel and a darling...'

'You'll turn my head,' said Sophie and laughed gently, 'but that's kind; thank you for the compliment.'

'You get enough of those from Rijk,' said Loewert and grinned again so that she blushed a little, remembering the things he had said to her before they married; nothing romantic, of course, but nice all the same. It was a pity that he hadn't found it necessary to repeat any of them now that they were married. It was as though they had slipped at once into a comfortable state of middle-aged marriage, and that within weeks...

She listened to Loewert's cheerful talk and wondered what she should do about it. She supposed that if she hadn't fallen in love with Rijk she would have been quite content to let their relationship dwindle into the state he seemed to want: pleasant companionship, a hostess for his table and complete lack of interest in his life. She loved him, though, which made it an entirely different matter. So something had to be done to remedy the matter, and she would do it...

'You do look fierce,' said Loewert. 'Have you got a headache?'

'No, no. I was trying to remember if Matt had his breakfast before he went with Rijk. So sorry; I was listening... You were telling me about the blonde nurse in Out-patients. Is she very pretty?'

The description of this blue-eyed paragon took some time. 'But of course I'm not serious,' he told her firmly.

'Time enough for all that when I've qualified and got established. I mean, look at old Rijk; plenty of girl-friends, mind you, but he never lost sight of the fact that he intended to be on top of the ladder before he settled down for good.' He sighed. 'If I'm half as good as he is when I'm as old, I'll be very satisfied.'

'Rijk isn't old,' protested Sophie.

'No, no, I know that—he's twelve years older than I am and eight years older than Iwert, who's doing quite well for himself. I suppose Rijk's the goal we are both aiming for.' He beamed at her confidingly. 'He's made a name for himself.'

'I'm sure you'll succeed. Are you going to specialise?'

He plunged into a rose-coloured version of his future. 'Though I'll never be as good at it as Rijk.' He smiled rather shyly. 'But I hope I meet someone as beautiful as you and marry her.'

'Why, thank you, Loewert—she'll be a lucky girl.' She got to her feet. 'Shall we have a short walk before lunch? Rijk says it will snow...'

They took the lane down to the lake and stood looking at its grey, cold water. 'It's certainly going to snow,' said Loewert. 'Look at those clouds.'

They were massing on the horizon, a nasty grey with a yellowish tinge sweeping towards them, driven by a mean wind.

They didn't stay out long but went back to the house and had lunch together on the best of terms.

They were playing draughts on the discarded tea-tray beside Sophie's chair when Rijk got home. She looked up and smiled as he came into the room, and he bent to kiss her cheek before greeting his brother.

'I've had a wonderful day,' said Loewert. 'I had no idea that a sister-in-law could be such fun. I hope I'll be invited again...'

'Any time you like,' said Rijk. 'Stay to dinner?'

'I promised Mother that I'd go home. I'd better go now or she may think I've forgotten.'

Sophie got up too and he kissed her with obvious pleasure. 'Next time I'll stay for dinner if you'll have me,' he told her.

'I've enjoyed our day together; pass your exams and we'll have a celebration dinner.'

Rijk went out of the room with him and she sat down again and picked up her knitting, presenting a picture of serene domesticity to Rijk when he came back to the room.

He said quietly, 'I'm glad you enjoyed your day; Loewert is great fun. Did you have time to look through the invitations?'

'Yes, I did, and there is a note from your mother asking us to go to dinner next week.'

'The entire family will be there—aunts and uncles and cousins, and, of course, Grandmother. Which reminds me—I've opened an account for you at my bank; maybe you will want to buy clothes.' He gave her a cheque-book and she turned it over slowly and then looked inside. It was very like her own cheque-book, save for the sum of money written on its first stub.

'Your quarterly allowance,' said Rijk, watching her. 'If you need more money you have only to ask.'

'That's a fortune.' She raised troubled eyes to his.

'You will need every cent of it; it won't do for you to be seen too often in the same dress. You dress charmingly, Sophie, but I can't have my friends saying that I don't give you enough pin money.' He smiled at her. 'Do you want to shop in London or den Haag? I'll make some time to go with you.'

'No, no, there are some lovely shops in Leeuwarden. I'll have a good look round. I have brought one or two dresses with me, but perhaps they aren't grand enough.'

He crossed the room and took her hands in his. 'They don't have to be grand, my dear, but there will be tea-parties and coffee-parties and several dinner parties we cannot refuse. You don't like dressing up?'

'I've never had much chance to do that.' She smiled up into his face. 'But I think I shall enjoy it as long as it's not too often.'

'I'll promise you that. I'm not very social myself, only, now that I have a wife, friends and acquaintances are going to invite us.'

Rauke came in then to take away the tray, and Matt, who had been having his supper in the kitchen, came with him, delighted to see Sophie again, rolling his yellow eyes at the prospect of his evening walk.

'I'll come with you,' said Sophie and, wrapped in an elderly loden cloak kept in the hall closet, went out into the dark evening. The cold hit her like a blow, and Rijk took her arm.

'I said that it would snow,' he said with satisfaction as the first feathery flakes fell.

They walked fast down towards the lake and back again while Matt, impervious to the cold in his thick coat, dashed to and fro, barking. He had a deep, very loud bark.

They went back indoors presently to eat their dinner and discuss which of the invitations they should accept. Afterwards, back in the drawing-room, leafing through them once again, Sophie asked, 'Who is Irena van Moeren? She's written a little note at the bottom, but I don't know what it means.'

'Irena? A very old friend; we must certainly accept.' He stretched out a hand for the card. 'She writes at the bottom, "You must come for old times' sake".' He glanced at the date. 'I must make a point of being free—you'll like her.'

Sophie murmured a gentle reply; she would hate her. Old times' sake, indeed ... And what if she turned out to be the woman she had seen Rijk with?

She sat, the picture of tranquillity, stitching away at her tapestry, not looking at him. If she had done so she would have been surprised to see the look on his face as he watched her.

It was snowing hard when she got up the next morning, and there was already a thick layer covering the lawn and shrubs. She went down to breakfast presently and was met in the hall by Rauke.

His 'Good morning' was grave and fatherly. 'The professor left early, *mevrouw*; he was called to an urgent case at four o'clock this morning.'

'He is operating this morning too; the list starts at nine o'clock. I do hope he gets some breakfast...'

'I'm sure that he will be looked after, *mevrouw*. I'll bring the coffee; you must have your breakfast.'

As he set the pot before her Sophie asked, 'Rauke, you speak such good English—have you been there?'

'No, *mevrouw*. I was with the professor's father during the occupation—underground, of course; we had a good deal to do with escaped prisoners and Secret Service personnel.'

She put out an impulsive hand. 'Oh, Rauke, I'm proud to know you.'

He took her hand gravely. 'Thank you, *mevrouw*. Would you care for a boiled egg?'

She was finishing breakfast with Matt in loving attendance when Rijk telephoned.

'Good morning, Sophie; you slept well?'

'Me? Slept? Oh, yes, thank you.' Ungrammatical and incoherent; she must do better. 'Are you tired? Was the op a success?'

'Yes, I think so; the next forty-eight hours will determine that.'

'Have you had breakfast?'

'Oh, yes.' She fancied that he was laughing. 'I'm going to scrub in a few minutes. If you go out, be careful, wear wellies—there are several pairs in the outer kitchen—and do take Matt with you.'

'Well, yes, I will. Will you be home in time for tea?' She did her best to make her voice sound brisk and friendly.

'Doubtful; I'll let you know later.' He rang off and she put the receiver down slowly. It was ridiculous to want to cry about nothing. She gave a sniff and blew her beautiful nose and went along to the kitchen to start the difficult but interesting business of deciding what to eat for the rest of the day.

It started to snow while she was out with Matt and she was glad of the wellies, for it was freezing now and the ground was icy. She walked down to the lake and took the track running beside it, which would lead her eventually to the village. The water, grey and sullen, reflected heavy cloud which covered the skies, and here and there there were great patches of ice forming.

'A winter's day and no mistake,' said Sophie to Matt, 'and I rather like it; it's like being in a Bruegel painting.'

In the village she bought stamps and a bar of chocolate in the small, crowded shop, exchanging greetings in her awkward Dutch, wishing she knew more words and making do with smiles and nods. The shop's owner was an old woman dressed severely in black, her hair dragged back in a severe bun, bright blue eyes almost hidden in her wrinkled face. She chattered away, not minding that Sophie understood one word in twenty, but she was friendly and when other customers came into the shop they all had a few words to say. Sophie went on her way feeling as though she belonged, munching chocolate. Matt munched too, keeping close to her as they took the narrow road to the house.

Rijk phoned late in the afternoon. It was snowing hard now and Rauke had drawn the heavy curtains across the windows, shutting out the dark early evening. Sophie, conning her Dutch phrase book, snatched the phone from its cradle. 'Rijk, when will you be home?'

He sounded placid. 'Very late, I'm afraid. I may have to operate again shortly. I'll get something to eat here. Don't wait up. What have you done with your day?'

'Well, I went for a long walk with Matt by the lake and then to the village and this afternoon I wrote letters and knitted.'

How dull it sounded; she was fast turning into an idle woman, and he would get bored with her. She said urgently, 'I should like to start Dutch lessons...'

'I'll see about it—I know the very person to teach you. What are you knitting?'

He sounded so kind that she felt the tears pricking her eyelids.

'A sweater for you,' she mumbled.

'That's the best thing I've heard all day,' he observed and with a brief '*Tot ziens*' rang off.

He was already sitting at the table when she went down to breakfast the next morning. His 'Good morning' was cheerful as he stood up and pulled out the chair opposite his.

Sophie sat down and poured her coffee. 'Were you very late?' she asked. She had waited until she had heard his footsteps soon after eleven o'clock, but she wasn't going to say so.

'Later than I had intended; the snow is piling up in the country roads, although the main roads are clear for the moment.'

'Oh—is it going to snow still?'

'Yes, and the temperature has dropped; we shall be skating by the end of the week.' He passed his cup for more coffee. 'Don't attempt to go on the lake, Sophie. The ice looks solid enough, but it isn't safe yet.'

'Will you be home for dinner this evening?' She added quickly, 'I only want to know so that Tyske can plan her cooking.'

'I should be home around six o'clock, so tell Tyske to go ahead. You should receive a phone call some time this afternoon from Mevrouw Smit, who will give you lessons in Dutch.'

'Oh, good, thank you, Rijk. Will she come here or shall I go to her?'

'You can arrange that between you. There will be a car for you in a few days, although I suggest that you wait for the weather to improve before you drive yourself; the roads are very bad at the moment.'

He dropped a hand on her shoulder as he went, but he didn't kiss her. Sophie gave Matt the rest of her toast and went along to the kitchen. To keep busy was important. She would answer their invitations during the morning and take Matt for a walk after lunch. There was the family dinner party to think about too...

The snow stopped during the morning and after lunch she wrapped herself in her top coat, tugged a woolly cap over her head, put on the thick gloves she had prudently bought in Leeuwarden, and began to walk briskly towards the village with Matt. It was slippery underfoot and very cold but the air was exhilarating and when she reached the village the few shops had their lights on and those people she saw called a greeting to her. There were lights on in the one hotel too; she supposed that if there was a good deal of skating, they would have plenty of custom. It was a sports centre, even if it was a small one.

Matt expected chocolate; she bought a bar and, since it was still reasonably light, decided to walk back along the track by the lake.

The water had become ice overnight; it looked solid enough but she remembered what Rijk had said. Once it was pronounced safe she supposed the whole lake

would be crowded with skaters; he had told her that she
would find it easy to skate, but she felt doubtful about
that. The lake looked cold and vast and very lonely in
the gathering gloom.

The track curved away from the water for a short distance and then turned back to the lake, and now she
could see the lights from the house; in a few minutes she
would go through the little wooden gate which led to
the grounds. There would be tea waiting and perhaps a
phone call from Rijk...

High-pitched shrieks brought her to an abrupt halt;
there were children ahead of her, standing dangerously
near the edge of the lake and screaming; they sounded
excited until one of them darted on to the ice and started
to run.

Sophie ran too; she had reached them when the ice
cracked and the small figure disappeared. The children
were silent now, dumb with shock, and she turned to
the nearest. 'Help!' she shouted, and then, gathering her
sparse vocabulary together, added urgently in Dutch, 'Go
and get help! Quick!'

The child, a small boy of six or seven, gave her a
frightened look and ran off and the others followed him
as she took off her coat and boots and started across
the lake; it gave at once under her weight, and Matt,
slithering and slipping beside her, sent up great splashes
of icy water. The child was standing now, the water up
to his chest, shrieking his head off and not moving, and
when she reached him he stopped his screams, his small
face bluish with cold and his teeth rattling. She put an
arm, heavy with freezing water, around him. 'Come on.'

She tried to smile from a face rigid with cold. 'We can get back easily.'

He didn't move, however, and she realised that in a few minutes she would be in like case; the numbness was already creeping into her legs and in a very short time she wouldn't be able to use them.

Matt had kept close to her, uncertain but willing, and now she said, 'Fetch the master, Matt. Hurry—the master.'

He didn't like to leave her, but he went, plunging through the broken ice and racing away, jumping the gate and tearing up to the house. She watched him go, and then, fighting the bitter cold, she took a deep breath and started to scream for help. It was a quiet evening and surely someone would hear her.

Rijk had just stopped in front of his door when Matt reached him and he said sharply, 'You're soaked—you've been in the lake.' He put out a hand, but Matt shook it off, barking furiously and then turning and running back round the house, to appear a moment later, still barking, dancing impatiently round Rijk, then running off again.

The professor was a fit man despite his vast size; he ran as fast as Matt, vaulted the gate, and came to a halt by the lake in time to hear Sophie's shouts. Matt was already in the water; Rijk tossed off his coat and waded in after him. The water was already freezing over...

It wasn't far but it was hard going, for the ground was a slithering mud. When he reached her he put an arm round her. 'All right, my darling, we'll be out of here in no time...'

'Legs,' said Sophie through chattering teeth.

'I know. I'm going to put an arm round you both. Hold on to the child; it's only a few yards.'

They were halfway there when the first of the men arrived with torches and ropes. They waded into the water and, while one of them took the boy in his arms, the other one took Sophie's arm and between them he and Rijk half carried Sophie in to the bank.

The professor said something to the men, picked Sophie up and started towards the house, the man and the child with him, Matt panting beside him, while the second man ran ahead.

The door leading to the kitchen was open, light streaming from it and Rauke waiting there. The professor spoke to him and he went away to return within minutes with an armful of blankets. Moments later the child was being undressed by Tyske and one of the men and rolled into a blanket and Sophie, her sodden person swathed in yet more blankets, was laid carefully in one of the old-fashioned basket chairs by the Aga.

Rijk hadn't spoken; he went over to the child and Tyske took his place, taking off Sophie's stockings and rubbing her feet and legs with a towel. She talked soothingly as she did so and Sophie bit her lip, trying not to cry as life began to return to them.

She turned her head to see where the boy was and asked, '*De kind*? Is OK?' Tyske nodded and smiled and went on rubbing.

The kitchen seemed full of people; the boy's mother had been fetched and the child was sitting up now, drinking warm milk, still shaking and crying. The professor had been telephoning from a corner of the kitchen and the boy was sitting on his father's knee now, still crying.

Sophie looked up at Rijk as he came over to her. 'He's all right?'

'He's fine. I'm sending him to the cottage hospital at Grouw for the night—he can have a check-up there. His father can borrow the Land Rover.'

He smiled at her. 'I'm going to carry you up to your room and Tyske will help you have a warm bath and get to bed. One of the maids is getting you a warm drink.' His eyes searched her face. 'You'll feel better after a good night's sleep.'

'But you—you're cold and wet too.'

He stooped and dropped a kiss on to her wet head. 'All in good time.'

'Matt's all right?'

'Rauke's giving him a good rub down and a warm meal. He can come and see you presently.'

He scooped her up then and carried her upstairs, with Tyske trotting in front to open the door and throw a blanket over the bed.

'I'll be back,' he told her and went away.

Half an hour later she was in bed, blissfully warm once more, her newly washed hair tied back, sipping warm milk which Tyske brought her before she bustled round the room collecting discarded clothes and tidying up.

When Rijk knocked on the door Matt came in with him, coming to lean against the bed and stare at her, his tongue hanging out with pleasure.

'You splendid brave fellow,' said Sophie and rubbed his rough head in the way he liked best, glad of something to do, because she felt shy of Rijk, who had come to sit on the bed.

He took her hand, but only to feel her pulse, his manner impersonal but friendly. 'Feeling better?' he asked.

'I'm fine really. I feel a fraud lying here in bed.' She sat up straighter. 'Thank you, Rijk, for saving us—you were so quick. We really couldn't move, you know.'

He was still holding her hand. 'Cold, wasn't it?' He smiled at her.

'Very. You've changed? You're all right? And the boy?'

'Gone to Grouw to the hospital there for the night. His mother and father asked me to tell you that they would be indebted to you for the rest of their lives.'

'I was so frightened . . .'

'Which makes you doubly brave.' He laid her hand on the coverlet. 'You'll eat your supper in bed and then go to sleep.' He got up, towering over her. 'I'll look in later just to make sure that you are asleep.'

'You don't have to go anywhere? You'll be here?'

'I'll be here.' He went quietly, with Matt crowding at his heels.

Anneke, one of the housemaids, brought her supper presently: soup, creamed chicken, potatoes whipped to an unbelievable lightness and a *crème brûlée* to finish off. She ate the lot with a splendid appetite and drank the glass of hock accompanying it and when Anneke came for the tray told her in awkward Dutch that she wanted nothing more.

The house was very quiet and the room pleasantly warm; the curtains drawn across the windows shut out the cold dark outside. Sophie closed her eyes and slept. Rijk, coming to see how she fared around midnight, stood for several minutes, looking down at her. She lay curled up in bed, her hands pillowing her cheek, her lovely mouth slightly open, so that there was no mistaking the faintest of snores. He bent and dropped a kiss on her head and then went away.

She was young and strong and healthy; she got up the next morning feeling none the worse for her ducking. She was halfway down the staircase on her way to breakfast when Rijk's voice stopped her. His study door was half open and he was on the phone and, hearing her own name, she stopped and listened.

He was speaking Dutch, but she understood a word here and there, enough to know that he was saying something about the accident at the lake. It was when he said, laughing, 'Oh, Irena,' that she stiffened. He had a rather slow, clear voice and she could pick out more words now. Something about this evening and dinner... He stopped speaking and she nipped smartly upstairs again, and then, as he came from his study and crossed the hall, she started down again. He looked up and saw her and they went into breakfast together.

'You're feeling perfectly fit?' he wanted to know. 'It might be a good idea if you stayed indoors today. I've a busy day ahead of me and, alas, I shan't be home for dinner, so have something and go to bed early.'

'Very well. Surely you aren't operating this evening?' She was pleased at her casual tone.

'No.' He stared at her across the table. 'An evening engagement with an old patient that I prefer not to put off. I can, of course, do so if you want me at home, but since you are looking quite yourself and it is a matter of some importance I should like to go.'

'No, no, of course you don't have to come home. I've so much to keep me occupied; the days are never long enough. Besides, Tiele is coming to tea.'

She gave him a dazzling smile. 'It would be silly of me to ask you to drive carefully, wouldn't it?'

He got up, ready to leave. 'Very silly, but rather nice too.' He touched her lightly as he went. 'Don't wait up,' he said casually as he went through the door.

CHAPTER NINE

SOPHIE sat at the table after Rijk had gone, feeding Matt pieces of toast while she thought. It had been wrong of her to eavesdrop, she knew that, but if she hadn't she wouldn't have known, would she? She wasn't sure what she did know, but it seemed likely that Rijk was still seeing someone—a woman—whom he had known and perhaps loved or been in love with before he met her and decided that she would fill the empty space he had allocated for a suitable wife. 'The heartless brute,' said Sophie in a stony little voice and, since she loved him with all her heart, not meaning a word of it.

She had told Rijk that she would stay indoors, but Matt had to go out; she put on the woolly cap and the loden cloak, stuck her feet into wellies, and took him for a brisk run in the grounds. The sky was still grey and the wind bitter, but the snow had stopped. When she got back to the house Rauke told her that tomorrow everyone would be skating.

Tiele came after lunch, bringing with her another young woman, a friend with whom she had been lunching and who had professed a keen desire to meet Rijk's bride. She was older than Tiele, tall and fair and with cold blue eyes, quite beautifully dressed. Sophie didn't like her and knew that she wasn't liked either, but on the surface at least they appeared good friends, and Tiele—kind, warm-hearted Tiele—noticed nothing, and there was plenty to talk about—the children, the family

171

dinner party, only two days away now, and finally
Elisabeth Willenstra's engagement.

'I shall have a big wedding,' she told Sophie, 'for we
have so many friends, Wim and I. You and Rijk must
come, of course—it will be in two months' time. Such
a pity that I shall be away for your party, but we're sure
to meet again—Rijk has so many friends.' She gave
Sophie a sharp glance. 'I expect you have met Irena—
Irena van Moeren—by now? One of his oldest friends.'

Sophie busied herself with the teapot. 'We haven't met
yet; there has hardly been time. We had an invitation——'

'I'm sure Rijk will have found time.'

There was so much spite in Elisabeth's voice that Tiele
looked up. 'If he has, it must have been by chance,' she
said, 'and I'm sure Sophie knows about her, anyway,
don't you, Sophie?'

'Oh, yes, of course,' said Sophie. It was surprising
how easily the lie tripped off her tongue. It was in a
good cause, she decided, for Elisabeth looked
disappointed.

Alone again, she allowed herself half an hour's worry
about the tiresome Irena. Elisabeth had been trying to
needle her; all the same, this Irena van Moeren was
someone to reckon with. Sophie decided that she would
feel much better if she met the woman...

Rijk was late home, which was a good thing, for
Sophie was in a bad temper and ripe for a quarrel.

The same bad temper prevented her from going to
Leeuwarden to look for a dress for the family party. She
would wear the pink she had bought in London. What
did it matter what she wore? she reflected pettishly, wall-

owing in a gloomy self-pity; no one would notice. And of course by no one she meant Rijk.

She had tried hard to forget Elisabeth Willenstra's sly remarks. All the same, she hadn't been very successful; Irena van Moeren was beginning to loom very large on her horizon, and she wished with all her heart that she didn't need to go to the family gathering.

There was to be a family dinner first before the guests arrived, and Rijk had come home early and spent half a hour with her in the drawing-room before they'd parted to dress, and now she was on the point of going downstairs.

The pink dress had lifted her spirits; it was pretty without being too girlish and flattered her splendid person. She had done her hair in its usual complicated coil, hooked in the diamond earrings, and fastened the pearl necklace; now she took a last look at her reflection in the pier-glass in her room and, catching up the mohair wrap to keep her warm on their journey, she went downstairs.

Rijk was in the drawing-room, standing by the open French window while Matt pranced around in the snow. Sophie, coming quietly into the room, thought that he was the handsomest man she had ever set eyes on; certainly a dinner-jacket, superbly cut, set off his massive proportions to the very best advantage.

He turned round at the soft sound of her skirt's rustle and studied her at his leisure. 'You look beautiful,' he said quietly.

She thanked him just as quietly; she had very little conceit, but she knew that she was looking her best. If only her best would match up to Irena van Moeren...

Matt came bounding in to stand obediently and have his great paws wiped clean before going to his basket, and Rijk said, 'If you are ready, I think we had better be on our way.'

He was perfectly at ease as they drove to Leeuwarden, telling her about his day's work, asking her what she had been doing, promising that since he was free on the following day he would take her on to the lake and give her her first skating lesson. She answered suitably in a voice so unlike her open manner that he asked her if she was nervous.

'You don't need to be,' he assured her. 'The family may be overpowering but they love you and, as for the guests, I'll be there to hold your hand.'

She said, 'You have so many friends, haven't you? I shan't remember any names, and will they all speak English?'

'Oh, yes. Although I expect Grandmother will make a point of addressing you in Dutch—she can be very contrary—although I have it from Mother that she approves of you, largely because you look as a woman should look.'

'You mean my clothes?'

'No, Sophie, your person. Your curves are generous and in the right places; she considers that a woman should look like one, not like a beanpole.' He glanced sideways at her in the dimness of the car. 'And I do agree with her, I certainly do.'

Her face flamed and she was glad that he couldn't see that. Her 'Thank you' was uttered in a prim voice which made him smile.

The whole family were waiting for them as they entered the drawing-room, and she was glad that she had

worn the pink dress; she felt comfortable in it and it
matched the other dresses there in elegance. Rijk had
taken her hand, going from one person to another after
they had greeted his parents, reminding her of names.
Aunts and uncles, cousins and the older nieces and
nephews, there seemed to be no end to them, but presently, after they had drunk their champagne and spoken
to everyone, she found herself at the dinner-table, sitting
on the right of her father-in-law, and thankfully Loewert
was on her other side. Rijk was at the other end of the
table, sitting beside his mother, and the meal was con-
ducted in a formal manner since it was, as her host assured her, a most important occasion in the family.

Dinner was lengthy and delicious and, between father
and son, Sophie began to enjoy herself. By the time they
rose and made their way back to the drawing-room she
felt quite at ease, and when Rijk joined her and slipped
an arm round her waist she smiled up at him, momen-
tarily forgetful of her worries, only to have them all
crowding back into her head as the guests began to arrive
and her foreboding was realised.

Irena van Moeren was one of the first to arrive and
she was indeed the woman Sophie had seen with Rijk;
moreover, she was a strikingly handsome one, not young
any more, but beautifully turned out in a black gown
of utter simplicity.

That she knew everyone there was obvious and when
she reached Rijk and Sophie she lifted her face for his
kiss in a way which made it plain that she had done it
many times before. She kissed Sophie too, and held her
hand, telling her how delighted she was to meet her. 'We
must become friends,' she said, and sounded as though
she really meant it.

If Rijk was in love with her, reflected Sophie, agreeing with false enthusiasm, then she couldn't blame him; Irena was charming and obviously kind and warm-hearted. If Sophie hadn't hated her so thoroughly, she would have liked her. There was no sign of her husband and she must either be married or a widow, for she wore a ring. Perhaps, thought Sophie, allowing her thoughts to wander, Rijk had been unable to marry her when her husband was alive, and, now that he was dead, he was married himself.

She became aware that Irena was saying something to her. 'Rijk has asked me to spend an afternoon with you both, skating on the lake.'

'I don't skate,' said Sophie bleakly. She would have to stand and watch the two of them executing complicated figures together...

'You'll learn in no time, Rijk on one side of you and me on the other.'

Rijk hadn't spoken; she summoned up an enthusiasm she didn't feel and said heartily, 'Oh, that sounds wonderful. Do come.' She glanced at Rijk, 'I'm not sure when you're free, but if you could bring Irena for lunch one day soon?'

He didn't remind her that he had already told her that he was free on the following day. 'Tomorrow? I'll fetch you, Irena; we'll have an early lunch so that we can get the best of the afternoon.'

'Oh, yes,' Sophie added, 'and stay for dinner; I shall look forward to it.'

They were joined by several other guests then and it wasn't until the end of the evening that Sophie spoke to Irena again. She had come over to say goodbye and

Sophie said gaily, 'Don't forget tomorrow—I do look forward to it.'

They were the last to leave; the family had stayed for a little while after the last of the guests had gone, mulling over the evening and then going home, until only Rijk's brothers and parents were left.

'It was a perfectly lovely evening,' declared Sophie, kissing and being kissed. 'Thank you very much. I—I feel one of the family now and I hope you will let me be that.'

Mevrouw van Taak ter Wijsma embraced her with warmth. 'You dear child, you have been one of us since the moment we saw you. I look forward to a delightful future with my new daughter. You are so exactly right for Rijk.'

Sophie smiled; of course she was right for Rijk, but did he think so too? Was she to be second best in his life? He would be good to her and care for her as his wife, but would he always be eating his heart out for Irena?

If he were, he showed no signs of it as they drove back home. It was a clear night with a bright moon, turning the snow-clad countryside to a fairytale beauty; he talked about their evening and the various people who had been there, apparently not noticing her silence. Only when they got home did he remark that it had been an exciting evening for her and that she must be tired. 'Go to bed, my dear,' he told her, 'and get some sleep. You have no need to get up for breakfast—I'll fetch Irena about midday and I'm sure that Tyske will cope with lunch.'

A remark which brought her out of her silence. 'It was a lovely evening and I am a little tired, but I don't want to stay in bed in the morning. Since you aren't going to the hospital in the morning perhaps we might have breakfast a little later, though?'

'Of course; tell Rauke before you go to bed. Would you like coffee or tea now?'

She shook her head, wished him goodnight, had a word with Rauke, and went to her room. She undressed slowly and got into bed and lay awake long after the house was quiet. The thought of the hours she must spend in Irena's company made her feel quite sick. She slept at last, to dream that Irena had come to the house, accompanied by piles of luggage, and that she herself was transported, in the way of dreams, on to an icy waste and told to skate back to England. It took her all of half an hour, using all her common sense, to face the grey light of early morning.

She got up thankfully and dressed carefully, wishing that she had gone to Leeuwarden as Rijk had suggested and bought some new clothes. She got into corduroy trousers and a heavy sweater and was rewarded by Rijk's genial, 'Ah, all ready to skate, I see.' He had given her face, pinched by worry and lack of sleep, a quick look. 'It should be excellent on the lake; there's not much wind. I've been down to have a look and there's plenty of hard, smooth ice, just right for you.' He added kindly, 'Of course, if you don't feel like it, you have no need to skate today—there will be ice for some time, I should think.'

She took a reviving sip of coffee. The idea of allowing him and Irena to spend half the day on the lake was sufficient to make her doubly keen to skate; jealousy was a great incentive, she had just discovered, although she despised herself for giving way to it. She said airily,

'Oh, but I'm longing to learn—I must be the only person living in Friesland who can't skate.'

He laughed then and began to talk about other things and presently went away to his study to emerge in time to take Matt for a walk before he went to fetch Irena.

Sophie, making sure that lunch was going to be ready by the time they returned, wondered how she was going to get through the day.

Standing at the window, she watched the car stop before the house and Irena and Rijk get out. Irena was laughing, obviously happy, and looking eye-catching in a scarlet anorak and stretch leggings, a scarf, tied with careless elegance, over her blonde hair.

Sophie went into the hall to meet them, the very picture of a smiling and delighted hostess, hurrying her guest away to take off her jacket and tidy herself, keeping up a flow of chat in a manner so unlike her that Rijk, getting drinks for them all, turned away to hide a smile, at the same time puzzled as to her manner...

With Matt in delighted attendance, they went down to the lake in the early afternoon and Rijk fastened skates on to Sophie's boots. They were broad and, she was assured, just right for a learner. He and Irena put on a quite different skate, specially used in Freisland and very fast.

Once on the ice Sophie did her best, held firmly on either side, sliding and slipping, until Rijk said, 'You're doing splendidly; lean forward a little and don't think about your feet. Irena is going to let go of you in a moment, but you won't fall; I have you safe.'

She didn't fall; the sight of Irena, skimming away with casual grace, inspired her to keep on her feet and presently she said, 'I believe I could go alone; may I try?'

She struck out bravely, letting out small screams of delight as she went forward. 'Look, look,' she called to Rijk. 'I'm skating; I can——'

The next moment she was tottering, waving her arms wildly in an effort to keep her balance as Rijk put a bracing arm around her and stood her upright again.

'That was splendid,' he observed, but Sophie, floundering around trying to regain her balance, could see Irena gliding gracefully back with an effortless ease which did nothing to improve Sophie's self-confidence.

'Sophie—but how splendid, you were skating alone. Never mind that you lost your balance; in a few days you will be good. Rijk, I will stay with Sophie while you take a turn around the lake.'

Of course Rijk had every right to go off on his own, but did he need to go so willingly, with nothing but a nod and a smile for her? She watched him race away, his hands clasped behind his back, moving effortlessly.

'He's very good,' said Irena. 'He has taken part in our *Elfstedentocht* several times, and twice he has won. It is a great test for a skater, for they must skate on the canals and waterways between eleven towns in Friesland.'

'I suppose he was taught when he was a little boy.'

'Yes, we all skate almost as soon as we can walk; we all learned together, but he was always the best of us.' She put a firm arm under Sophie's elbow. 'Now let us continue... Strike out with your right foot, so. Good, now do it with your left foot, and again, faster... You know about Rijk and us...?'

She spoke very quietly and when Sophie shot her a glance she looked sad.

'Yes,' said Sophie; she looked to where Rijk was tearing back across the ice.

'Good, then we do not need to speak of it; it is for me very sad.' She became brisk once more. 'Now if you will go alone, and if you fall I shall pick you up.'

If only she could go somewhere quiet and have a good cry, thought Sophie despairingly, but she was quite unable to deal with her wretched skates, and anyway, what would be the use? How much easier it would be if she could hate Irena, even dislike her a little, but she liked her; she could quite see why Rijk loved her. She plunged forward, not caring if she fell and broke a leg or an arm, and to her great surprise she kept on her feet for several yards until she was neatly fielded by Rijk, back again.

'You're an excellent pupil,' she was told, 'but that's enough for today; let us go home and have tea.'

'Wouldn't you and Irena like to skate together? I don't mind a bit; if you would take off my skates I'll go on ahead and make sure tea is ready.'

He gave her a quick look, his eyes thoughtful. 'We've had enough, haven't we, Irena? We'll have tea and then I'll take you back.'

'I thought Irena was staying for dinner?' Anyone would think, reflected Sophie, that I am enjoying this conversation.

'I did tell Rijk; I'm so sorry that I didn't tell you too——' Irena looked quite crestfallen '—but I have an appointment this evening and it is important that I should be there. Forgive me, Sophie.'

'Well, of course; you must come another time. We'll have tea round the fire...'

Which they did, with Matt crouching beside his master, accepting any morsel which might come his way, and the talk was all of skating and how well Sophie had done, and presently Irena said that she really must go.

Sophie, the hospitable hostess even though it was killing her, murmured regret and the wish that they might meet again soon, and waved them away from the porch, Matt beside her, puzzled as to why he wasn't going too. Sophie was puzzled as well; after all, Rijk was only driving into Leeuwarden and back again.

The pair of them went back to the fireside, Matt to snooze and she to sit and worry. It had been a horrendous day; she had been hopelessly outclassed on the ice and Irena's calm acceptance of the situation had left her uncertain and unhappy. She was deeply hurt too that Rijk hadn't talked to her about it. After all, it could happen to anyone, and she was fair enough to realise that to have been in love, perhaps for years, with each other with no hope of marrying and then to find the way clear, only for Rijk to have married someone else in the meantime, must be a terrible thing to happen. Was Irena's husband dead, she wondered, or were they divorced? When Rijk came home she would ask him; after all, they were the best of friends and should be able to discuss the problem without rancour.

She gave a great sigh and Matt opened his eyes and grunted worriedly. 'I think my heart is broken,' said Sophie. 'It would be so simple if only I didn't love him.'

Matt got up and laid his great head on her lap and presently, when she went upstairs to change her dress, even went with her. He wasn't allowed in the bedrooms, but she sensed that he was disobeying out of kindness. She put on one of her prettiest dresses, took pains with her face and hair, and went downstairs to wait for Rijk.

Only he didn't come. It wanted only a few minutes to dinner when the phone rang.

'Sophie.' Rijk's voice sounded urgently in her ear. 'I shall be delayed. Don't wait dinner and don't wait up.'

'Yes,' said Sophie and hung up. It had been an inadequate answer; she might have said, 'I quite understand,' or even, 'Very well.'

She dined alone with Rauke serving her and taking away the almost uneaten plates of food with a worried air. She saw the look and said hastily, 'I'm not hungry, Rauke; it must be all that skating. If the professor isn't back by eleven o'clock will you lock up, please, and leave the door for him and something in the kitchen? He may be cold and hungry. He didn't say when he would be home, but it sounded urgent.'

She added that last bit to make it sound convincing, even though in her mind's eye she could see Rijk and Irena spending the evening together. With a mythical headache as an excuse, she went to bed early.

She didn't sleep; it was almost two o'clock when she heard Rijk's quiet tread on the stairs. Only then did she fall into a troubled sleep.

He was already at the table when she went down to breakfast in the morning.

'Don't get up,' she told him sharply. 'I dare say you're tired after your short night.' Then, because she was beside herself with lack of sleep and unhappiness and worry, she allowed her tongue to say things she had never meant to utter.

'I'm only surprised that you bothered to come home, but of course you weren't to know that I know all about it.'

She stopped then, otherwise she might have burst into tears, and poured herself a cup of coffee with a shaking hand. After a heartening sip, she added, 'You might have told me.'

The professor sat back in his chair, watching her. He was bone-weary, after operating for hours, but his voice was placid enough as he asked, 'And why should I not come home, Sophie? I live here.'

Sophie mauled the slice of toast on her plate. 'Bah.' Her voice shook. 'I've just told you, I know about you and Irena...'

The professor didn't move. 'And?' he asked in an encouraging voice.

'Well, are we supposed to go on like this for the rest of our lives? Elisabeth Willenstra said——'

'Ah—Elisabeth.' His voice was quiet, but his blue eyes were hard.

'Well, that you and Irena were old friends... She didn't say anything in so many words, but I can take a hint. Besides——' she gulped back tears and went on steadily '—that evening I came back by bus—I had gone to the hospital to go home with you. It was as I was waiting to cross the street opposite the entrance that I saw you both coming out together. She looked so happy and you were smiling at her and holding her arm and...yesterday Irena asked if I knew about you... Those were her words—"You know about Rijk and us?"—and of course I said yes.' She could hear her voice getting louder and shrill, but she couldn't stop now. 'And you stayed out almost all night and she was coming to dinner but then she said she had to go back and you went with her.'

The professor still hadn't moved. 'You believe that I would do this to you?'

Something in his calm voice made her mumble, 'You can't help falling in love, can you? I mean, when you do it matters more than anything else, doesn't it?'

'Indeed it does. I see no point in continuing this conversation at the moment. I shall be late home; don't wait up.'

He was at the door when she asked in a small voice, 'Are you very angry, Rijk?'

He turned to look at her. He wasn't just tired, he was white with anger, his eyes blazing.

'Dangerously so, Sophie,' he said and went away, closing the door softly behind him.

She wished with all her heart that she had held her tongue.

She took Matt for a walk presently, in the cold stillness of the icy morning, and she was able to think clearly. She would have to apologise, of course, and ask to be forgiven, although it was she who should be doing the forgiving, and she would insist on a sensible discussion. They had always been good friends, able to talk easily and communicate with each other. It was a great pity that she had fallen in love with him; it was a complication she hadn't envisaged.

She went back home and made a pretence of eating the lunch Rauke had ready for her and then wandered around the house, unable to settle to anything. She was in the small sitting-room, looking unseeingly out of the window, when Rauke announced Irena.

Sophie pinned a smile on her face and turned to welcome her guest. Rijk would have seen her, of course, and she had come to explain...

Irena came in with an outstretched hand. 'Sophie, I am on my way back to Leeuwarden and I thought I would come and see you. You don't mind?'

Sophie took the hand. 'Of course not. I expect you've seen Rijk?'

Irena looked puzzled. 'Rijk?' She frowned. 'No.' She looked suddenly anxious. 'He has telephoned here? He would like to speak to me urgently?' She had gone quite white. 'Jerre—he is not so well... I must telephone... He was improving; what can have happened?'

She sounded distraught and Sophie said, 'Who is Jerre?'

'My husband—you knew? You said that you did. He had a brain tumour and Rijk saved his life, but we told no one because Jerre is director of a big business concern and if it were known that he was so very ill it would have caused much panic and shareholders would have lost money... but I must telephone.'

'It's all right, Irena, I'm sure your husband is all right. It's just that I thought that you might have seen Rijk. It's just that I didn't know about your husband.'

Irena was no fool. 'Oh, my poor dear, you thought Rijk and I... He is Jerre's best friend; we all grew up together. Why should you think that of us?'

'Someone called Elisabeth...'

'That woman... She pretends to be everyone's friend, but she is spiteful; she likes to make trouble. Nothing of what she said to you is true; you must believe me.'

'I do, only I've quarrelled with Rijk, and, you see, I'm in love with him and he doesn't know that. I can't explain...'

'No, no,' said Irena soothingly, 'a waste of time. Get your coat and hat and come to Leeuwarden with me. He will be at the hospital; you must find him there and explain to him. He is angry, yes? He has a nasty temper, but he controls it. Tell him you love him.'

Sophie shook her head. 'I can't do that; if I do I shall have to leave him . . .'

'You must do what you think is best, but I do beg you, get your coat.'

Irena dropped her off outside the hospital, kissed her warmly, and waited in the car until she saw Sophie through the doors.

The porter was in his little box. Seeing Sophie, he shook his head. 'The professor is not here, *mevrouw.*' His English was surprisingly good. 'He is gone.'

'But his car is outside.'

'He holds his clinic five minutes away from here; he walks.'

'Will you tell me where the clinic is?'

The directions were complicated and she wasn't sure if she had them right, but she had wasted enough time already. She thanked him and he said, 'The clinic lasts until five o'clock; you should hurry, *mevrouw.*'

She hurried, trying to remember his directions, but after five minutes' walking she knew that she had gone wrong; the street she was in was narrow, lined with old houses and run-down shops, and it didn't appear to have a name. A matronly woman was coming towards her and Sophie stopped her, gathered together the best of her Dutch, and asked the way. Precious moments were lost while she repeated everything under the woman's beady eyes.

'*Engelse*?' she wanted to know, and, when Sophie nodded, broke into a flood of talk, not a word of which Sophie understood. She was wasting time. When the woman paused for breath, Sophie thanked her politely and hurried on. There was a crossroads ahead, not a main street, but it might lead somewhere where she could ask again. She was in a quite nasty temper by now; she was lost and unhappy and she was never going to find Rijk, and that was more important than anything else in the world. She shot round a corner head first into a broad expanse of cashmere overcoat.

'What a delightful surprise,' said Rijk, wrapping both arms around her.

'So there you are,' said Sophie in a very cross voice. 'I've been looking for you.' And she burst into tears.

Rijk stood patiently, rock-solid, while she sniffed and wept and muttered into his huge shoulder. Presently he took a very large white handkerchief from a pocket, still holding her close with his other arm, and mopped her face gently.

'Have a good blow and stop crying and tell me why you were looking for me.'

'I didn't mean a word of it,' said Sophie wildly. 'I've been mean and jealous and silly and I'm so ashamed and I can't skate and you only want us to be friends——' she gave a great sniff '—but I can't because I've fallen in love with you and I'll have to go away; I really can't go on like this.'

'My darling wife, I have been waiting patiently to hear you say that.' He smiled in the darkness. 'Ever since the moment I first saw you standing on the pavement outside St Agnes's and fell in love with you.'

'Then why didn't you say so?'

'My dear love, you weren't even sure if you liked me.'

She thought this over. 'But you do love me? You were so angry this morning that I didn't know what to do, but Irena came to see me and told me about Jerre and I came to say that I was sorry.'

'What a delightfully brave wife I have. Have you any idea where you are?'

'No, the porter told me where to go, but I couldn't understand him.'

He gave a rumble of laughter. 'However, you found me.' He bent his head and kissed her soundly. 'I shall always take care of you, my darling love.'

He did kiss her again, and an old man, shuffling past, shouted something and laughed.

'What did he say?' asked Sophie.

Rijk said gravely, 'Translated into polite English, he begged me to kiss and hug you.'

Sophie lifted her face to his. 'Well, hadn't you better take his advice?'